T0112445

CHARLES BUKOWSKI

THE CAPTAIN IS OUT TO LUNCH AND THE SAILORS HAVE TAKEN OVER THE SHIP

ILLUSTRATED BY ROBERT CRUMB

ecco

An Imprint of HarperCollinsPublishers

HarperCollins books may be purchased for educational, business, or sales promotional use. For information, please e-mail the Special Markets Department at - SPsales@harpercollins.com.

First Ecco edition 2002
Previously published by Black Sparrow Press

     THE Library of Congress has catalogued a previous edition as follows:
Bukowski, Charles, 1920-1994.
   The Captain is out to Lunch and the Sailors Have Taken Over the Ship / Charles Bukowski.
     p. cm.
   I. Crumb, Robert, 1943–
   ISBN 1-57423-058-1 (paper)
   ISBN 1-57423-059-X (cloth trade)
   I. Title.
IN PROCESS
818'.5403—dc21   98-4623
[B]   CIP

23 24 25 26 27 LBC 27 26 25 24 23

THE CAPTAIN

IS OUT TO LUNCH

AND THE SAILORS

HAVE TAKEN OVER

THE SHIP

Good day at the track, damn near swept the card.

Yet it gets boring out there, even when you're winning. It's the 30 minute wait between races, your life leaking out into space. The people look gray out there, walked through. And I'm there with them. But where else could I go? An Art Museum? Imagine staying home all day and playing at writer? I could wear a little scarf. I remember this poet who used to come by on the bum. Buttons off his shirt, puke on his pants, hair in eyes, shoelaces undone, but he had this long scarf which he kept very clean. That signaled that he was a poet. His writing? Well, forget it....

Came in, swam in the pool, then went to the spa. My soul is in danger. Always has been.

Was sitting on the couch with Linda, the good dark night descending, when there was a knock on the door. Linda got it.

"Better come here, Hank ..."

I walked to the door, barefooted, in my robe. A young blond guy, a young fat girl and a medium sized girl.

"They want your autograph ..."

"I don't see people." I told them.

"We just want your autograph," said the blond guy, "then we promise never to come back."

Then he started giggling, and holding his head. The girls just stared.

"But none of you have a pen or even a piece of paper," I said.

"Oh," said the blond kid, taking his hands from his

7

head, "We'll come back again with a book! Maybe at a more proper time ..."

The bathrobe. The bare feet. Maybe the kid thought I was eccentric. Maybe I was.

"Don't come in the morning," I told them.

I saw them begin to walk off and I closed the door....

Now I'm up here writing about them. You've got to be a little hard with them or they'll swarm you. I've had some horrible experiences blocking that door. So many of them think that somehow you'll invite them in and drink with them all night. I prefer to drink alone. A writer owes nothing except to his writing. He owes nothing to the reader except the availability of the printed page. And worse, many of the doorknockers are not even readers. They've just heard something. The best reader and the best human is the one who rewards me with his or her absence.

Slow at the track today, my damned life dangling on the hook. I am there every day. I don't see anybody else out there every day except the employees. I probably have some malady. Saroyan lost his ass at the track, Fante at poker, Dostoevsky at the wheel. And it's really not a matter of the money unless you run out of it. I had a gambler friend once who said, "I don't care if I win or lose, I just want to gamble." I have more respect for money. I've had very little of it most of my life. I know what a park bench is, and the landlord's knock. There are only two things wrong with money: too much or too little.

I suppose there's always something out there we want to torment ourselves with. And at the track you get the feel of the other people, the desperate darkness, and how easy they toss it in and quit. The racetrack crowd is the world brought down to size, life grinding against death and losing. Nobody wins finally, we are just seeking a reprieve, a moment out of the glare. (Shit, the lighted end of my cigarette just hit one of my fingers as I was musing on this purposelessness. That woke me up, brought me out of this Sartre state!) Hell, we need humor, we need to laugh. I used to laugh more, I used to do everything more, except write. Now, I am writing and writing and writing, the older I get the more I write, dancing with death. Good show. And I think the stuff is all right. One day they'll say, "Bukowski is dead," and then I will be truly discovered and hung from stinking bright lampposts. So what? Immortality is the stupid invention of the living. You see what the racetrack does? It makes the lines roll. Lightning and luck. The last bluebird singing. Anything I say sounds fine because I gamble when I write. Too many are too careful. They study, they teach and they fail. Convention strips them of their fire.

I feel better now, up here on this second floor with the Macintosh. My pal.

And Mahler is on the radio, he glides with such ease, taking big chances, one needs that sometimes. Then he sends in the long power rises. Thank you, Mahler, I borrow from you and I can never pay you back.

I smoke too much, I drink too much but I can't write too much, it just keeps coming and I call for more and it arrives and mixes with Mahler. Sometimes I deliberately stop myself. I say, wait a moment, go to sleep or look at your 9 cats or sit with your wife on the couch. You're either at the track or with the Macintosh. And then I stop, put on the brakes, park the damned thing. Some people have written that my writing has helped them go on. It has helped me too. The writing, the horses, the 9 cats.

There's a small balcony here, the door is open and I can see the lights of the cars on the Harbor Freeway south, they never stop, that roll of lights, on and on. All those people. What are they doing? What are they thinking? We're all going to die, all of us, what a circus! That alone should make us love each other but it doesn't. We are terrorized and flattened by trivialities, we are eaten up by nothing.

Keep it going, Mahler! You've made this a wondrous night. Don't stop, you son-of-a-bitch! Don't stop!

10

I should cut my toenails. My feet have been hurting me for a couple of weeks. I know it's the toenails yet I can't find time to cut them. I am always fighting for the minute, I have time for nothing. Of course, if I could stay away from the racetrack I would have plenty of time. But my whole life has been a matter of fighting for one simple hour to do what I want to do. There was always something getting in the way of my getting to myself.

I should make a giant effort to cut my toenails tonight. Yes, I know there are people dying of cancer, there are people sleeping in the streets in cardboard boxes and I babble about cutting my toenails. Still, I am probably closer to reality than some slug who watches 162 baseball games a year. I've been in my hell, I'm still in my hell, don't feel superior. The fact that I am alive and 71 years old and babbling about my toenails, that's miracle enough for me.

I've been reading the philosophers. They are really strange, funny wild guys, gamblers. Descartes came along and said, these fellows have been talking pure crap. He said that mathematics was the model for absolute self-evident truth. *Mechanism.* Then Hume came along with his attack on the validity of scientific causal knowledge. And then came Kierkegaard: "I stick my finger into existence—it smells of nothing. Where am I?" And then along came Sartre who claimed that existence was absurd. I love these boys. They rock the world. Didn't they get headaches thinking that way? Didn't a rush of blackness roar between their teeth? When you take men like these and stack them

11

against the men I see walking along the street or eating in cafes or appearing upon a tv screen the difference is so great that something wrenches inside of me, kicking me in the gut.

I probably won't do the toenails tonight. I'm not crazy but I'm not sane either. No, maybe I'm crazy. Anyway, today, when daylight comes and 2 p.m. arrives it will be the first race of the last day of racing at Del Mar. I played every day, every race. I think I'll sleep now, my razor nails slashing at the good sheets. Good night.

No horses today. I feel strangely normal. I know why Hemingway needed the bullfights, it framed the picture for him, it reminded him of where it was and what it was. Sometimes we forget, paying gas bills, getting oil changes, etc. Most people are not ready for death, theirs or anybody else's. It shocks them, terrifies them. It's like a great surprise. Hell, it should never be. I carry death in my left pocket. Sometimes I take it out and talk to it: "Hello, baby, how you doing? When you coming for me? I'll be ready."

There's nothing to mourn about death any more than there is to mourn about the growing of a flower. What is terrible is not death but the lives people live or don't live up until their death. They don't honor their own lives, they piss on their lives. They shit them away. Dumb fuckers. They concentrate too much on fucking, movies, money, family, fucking. Their minds are full of cotton. They swallow God without thinking, they swallow country without thinking. Soon they forget how to think, they let others think for them. Their brains are stuffed with cotton. They look ugly, they talk ugly, they walk ugly. Play them the great music of the centuries and they can't hear it. Most people's deaths are a sham. There's nothing left to die.

You see, I need the horses, I lose my sense of humor. One thing death can't stand is for you to laugh at it. True laughter knocks the longest odds right on their ass. I haven't laughed for 3 or 4 weeks. Something is eating me alive. I scratch myself, twist, look about, trying to find it. The Hunter is clever. You can't see him. Or her.

13

This computer must go back into the shop. Won't bless you with the details. Some day I will know more about computers than the computers themselves. But right now this machine has me by the balls.

There are two editors I know who take great offense at computers. I have these two letters and they rail against the computer. I was very surprised about the bitterness in the letters. And the childishness. I am aware that the computer can't do the writing for me. If it could, I wouldn't want it. They both just went on too long. The inference being that the computer wasn't good for the soul. Well, few things are. But I'm for convenience, if I can write twice as much and the quality remains the same, then I prefer the computer. Writing is when I fly, writing is when I start fires. Writing is when I take death out of my left pocket, throw him against the wall and catch him as he bounces back.

These guys think you always have to be on the cross and bleeding in order to have soul. They want you half mad, dribbling down your shirt front. I've had enough of the cross, my tank is full of that. If I can stay off the cross, I still have plenty to run on. Too much. Let them get on the cross, I'll congratulate them. But pain doesn't create writing, a writer does.

Anyway, back into the shop with this and when these two editors see my work typewritten again they'll think, ah, Bukowski has his soul back. This stuff reads much better.

Ah, well, what would we do without our editors? Or better yet, what would they do without us?

14

The track is closed. There is no inter-track wagering with Pomona, damned if I'm going to make that damned hot drive. I'll probably end up with night racing at Los Alamitos. The computer is out of the shop once more but it no longer corrects my spelling. I've hacked at this machine trying to dig it out. Will probably have to phone the shop, will ask the fellow, "What do I do now?" And he will say something like, "You have to transfer it from your main disk to your hard disk." I'll probably end up erasing everything. The typewriter sits behind me and says, "Look, I'm still here."

There are nights when this room is the only place I want to be. Yet I get up here and I'm an empty husk. I know I could raise hell and dance words on this screen if I got drunk but I have to pick up Linda's sister at the airport tomorrow afternoon. She's coming for a visit. She's changed her name from Robin to Jharra. As women get older, they change their names. Many do, I mean. Suppose a man did that? Can you see me phoning somebody:

"Hey, Mike, this is Tulip."

"Who?"

"Tulip. Formerly Charles, but now Tulip. I will no longer answer to Charles."

"Fuck you, Tulip."

Mike hangs up ...

Getting old is very odd. The main thing is that you have to keep telling yourself, I'm old, I'm old. You see yourself in the mirror as you descend the escalator but you

15

don't look directly at the mirror, you give a little side glance, a wary smile. You don't look that bad, you look something like a dusty candle. Too bad, screw the gods, screw the game. You should have been dead 35 years ago. This is a little extra scenery, more peeks at the horror show. The older a writer is the better he should write, he's seen more, endured more, lost more, he's closer to death. The latter is the greatest advantage. And there's always the new page, that white page, 8 and ½ by 11. The gamble remains. Then you always remember a thing or two one of the other boys have said. Jeffers: "Be angry at the sun." All too wonderful. Or Sartre: "Hell is other people." Right on and through the target. I'm never alone. The best thing is to be alone but not quite alone.

To my right, the radio works hard bringing me more great classical music. I listen to 3 or 4 hours of this a night as I am doing other things, or nothing. It's my drug, it washes the crap of the day right out of me. The classical composers can do this for me. The poets, the novelists, the short story writers can't. A gang of fakes. There is something about writing that draws the fakes. What is it? Writers are the most difficult to take, on the page or in person. And they are worse in person than on the page and that's pretty bad. Why do we say "pretty bad"? Why not "ugly bad"? Well, writers are pretty bad and ugly bad. And we love to bitch about one another. Look at me.

About writing, I write basically the same way now as I did 50 years ago, maybe a little better but not much. Why did I have to reach the age of 51 before I could pay the rent with my writing? I mean, if I'm right and my writing is no different, what took so long? Did I have to wait for the

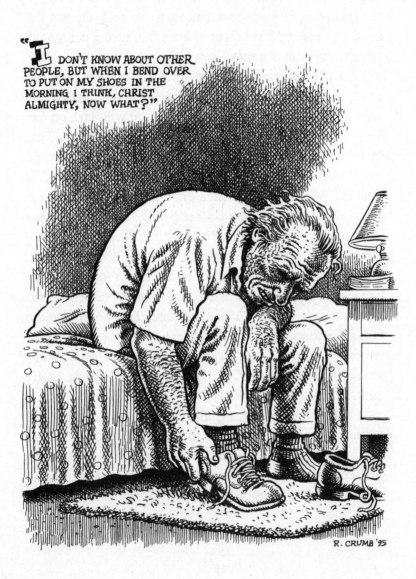

world to catch up with me? And now, if it has, where am I now? In bad shape, that's what. But I don't think I've gotten the fat head from any luck that I've had. Does a fathead ever realize that he's one? But I'm far from contented. Something is in me that I can't control. I can never drive my car over a bridge without thinking of suicide. I can never look at a lake or an ocean without thinking of suicide. I mean, I won't linger on it all. But it will flash on me: SUICIDE. Like a light going on. In the darkness. That there is an out helps you stay in. Get it? Otherwise, it could only be madness. And that's no fun, buddy. And whenever I get off a good poem, that's another crutch to keep me going. I don't know about other people, but when I bend over to put on my shoes in the morning, I think, Christ-oh-mighty, now what? I'm screwed by life, we don't get along. I have to take little bites out of it, not the whole thing. It's like swallowing buckets of shit. I am never surprised that the madhouses and jails are full and that the streets are full. I like to look at my cats, they chill me out. They make me feel all right. Don't put me in a roomful of humans, though. Don't ever do that. Especially on a holiday. Don't do it.

I heard they found my first wife dead in India and nobody in her family wanted the body. Poor girl. She had a crippled neck that couldn't turn. Other than that she was perfectly beautiful. She divorced me and she should have. I wasn't kind enough or big enough to save her.

Went to a movie premiere last night. Red carpet. Flash bulbs. Party afterwards. Two parties afterwards. Didn't hear much said. Too crowded. Too hot. First party I got cornered at the bar by a young guy with very round eyes who never blinked. I don't know what he was on. Or off. Quite a few people like that about. The young guy had 3 rather nice looking ladies with him and he kept telling me how they liked to suck cock. The ladies just smiled and said, "Oh, yes!" And the whole conversation went on like that. On and on like that. I kept trying to figure out whether it was true or whether I was being put on. But after a while I just got weary of it. But the young guy just kept pressing me, talking on about how the girls liked to suck cock. His face kept getting closer and he kept on and on. Finally, I reached out and grabbed him by his shirt front, hard, and held him like that and I said, "Listen, it wouldn't look good if a 71-year-old guy beat the shit out of you in front of all these people, would it?" Then I let go of him. He walked around the other end of the bar, fol-lowed by his ladies. Damned if I could make any sense out of it.

I guess I'm too used to sitting in a small room and making words do a few things. I see enough of humanity at the racetracks, the supermarkets, gas stations, freeways, cafes, etc. This can't be helped. But I feel like kicking myself in the ass when I go to gatherings, even if the drinks are free. It never works for me. I've got enough clay to play with. People empty me. I have to get away to refill. I'm

19

what's best for me, sitting here slouched, smoking a beedie and watching this screen flash the words. Seldom do you meet a rare or interesting person. It's more than galling, it's a fucking constant shock. It's making a god-damned grouch out of me. Anybody can be a god-damned grouch and most are. Help!

I just need a good night's sleep. But first, never a damned thing to read. After you've read a certain amount of decent literature, there just isn't any more. We have to write it ourselves. There's no juice in the air. But I expect to wake up in the morning. And the morning I don't, fine. I won't need any more window screens, razor blades, Racing Forms or message-taking machines. The phone rings mostly for my wife, anyhow. The Bells do not Toll for Me.

Sleep, sleep. I sleep on my stomach. Old habit. I've lived with too many crazy women. Got to protect the privates. Too bad that young guy didn't challenge me. I was in a mood to kick ass. Would have cheered me up immensely. Good night.

Hot stupid night, the cats are miserable, caught in all that fur, they look at me and I can't do anything. Linda off to a couple of places. She needs things to do, people to talk to. It's all right with me but she tends to drink and must drive home. I'm not good company, talking is not my idea of anything at all. I don't want to exchange ideas—or souls. I'm just a block of stone unto myself. I want to stay within that block, unmolested. It was that way from the beginning. I resisted my parents, then I resisted school, then I resisted becoming a decent citizen. It's like whatever I was, was there from the beginning. I didn't want anybody tinkering with that. I still don't.

I think that people who keep notebooks and jot down their thoughts are jerk-offs. I am only doing this because somebody suggested I do it, so you see, I'm not even an original jerk-off. But this somehow makes it easier. I just let it roll. Like a hot turd down a hill.

I don't know what to do about the racetrack. I think it's burning out for me. I was standing around at Hollywood Park today, inter-track betting, 13 races from Fairplex Park. After the 7th race I am $72 ahead. So? Will it take some of those white hairs out of my eyebrows? Will it make an opera singer out of me? What do I want? I am beating a difficult game, I am beating an 18 percent take. I do that quite a bit. So, it mustn't be too difficult. What do I want? I really don't care if there is a God or not. It doesn't interest me. So, what the hell is it about 18 percent?

I look over and see the same guy talking. He stands in

the same spot every day talking to this person or that or to a couple of people. He holds the Form and talks about the horses. How dreary! What am I doing here?

I leave. I walk down to parking, get in my car and drive off. It's only 4 p.m. How nice. I drive along. Others drive along. We are snails crawling on a leaf.

Then I get into the driveway, park, get out. There's a message from Linda taped to the phone. I check the mail. Gas bill. And a large envelope full of poems. All printed on separate pieces of paper. Women talking about their periods, about their tits and breasts and about getting fucked. Utterly dull. I dump it in the trash.

Then I take a dump. Feel better. Take off my clothes and step into the pool. Ice water. But great. I walk along toward the deep end of the pool, the water rising inch by inch, chilling me. Then I plunge below the water. It's restful. The world doesn't know where I am. I come up, swim to the far edge, find the ledge, sit there. It must be about the 9th or 10th race. The horses are still running. I plunge again into the water, being aware of my stupid whiteness, of my age hanging onto me like a leech. Still, it's o.k. I should have been dead 40 years ago. I rise to the top, swim to the far edge, get out.

That was a long time ago. I'm up here now with the Macintosh IIsi. And this is about all there is for now. I think I'll sleep. Rest up for the track tomorrow.

Got the proofs of the new book today. Poetry. Martin says it will run to about 350 pages. I think the poems hold up. Uphold. I am an old train steaming down the track.

Took me a couple of hours to read. I've had some practice at doing this thing. The lines roll free and say about what I want them to say. Now the main influence on myself is myself.

As we live we all get caught and torn by various traps. Nobody escapes them. Some even live with them. The idea is to realize that a trap is a trap. If you are in one and you don't realize it, then you're finished. I believe that I have recognized most of my traps and I have written about them. Of course, all of writing doesn't consist of writing about traps. There are other things. Yet, some might say that life is a trap. Writing can trap you. Some writers tend to write what has pleased their readers in the past. Then they are finished. Most writers' creative span is short. They hear the accolades and believe them. There is only one final judge of writing and that is the writer. When he is swayed by the critics, the editors, the publishers, the readers, then he's finished. And, of course, when he's swayed with his fame and his fortune, you can float him down the river with the turds.

Each new line is a beginning and has nothing to do with any lines which preceded it. We all start new each time. And, of course, it isn't all that holy either. The world can live much easier without writing than without plumbing. And some places in the world have very little of either.

Of course, I'd rather live without plumbing but I'm sick.

There's nothing to stop a man from writing unless that man stops himself. If a man truly desires to write, then he will. Rejection and ridicule will only strengthen him. And the longer he is held back the stronger he will become, like a mass of rising water against a dam. There is no losing in writing; it will make your toes laugh as you sleep; it will make you stride like a tiger; it will fire the eye and put you face to face with Death. You will die a fighter, you will be honored in hell. The luck of the word. Go with it, send it. Be the Clown in the Darkness. It's funny. It's funny. One more new line....

A title for the new book. Sat out at the track trying to think of one. That's one place where one can't think. It sucks the brains and spirit out of you. A draining blow job, that's what that place is. And I haven't been sleeping nights. Something is sapping the energy out of me.

Saw the lonely one at the track today. "How ya doin', Charles?" "O.k.," I told him, then drifted off. He wants camaraderie. He wants to talk about things. Horses. You don't talk about horses. That's the LAST thing you talk about. A few races went by and then I caught him looking at me over an automatic betting machine. Poor guy. I went outside and sat down and a cop started talking to me. Well, they call them security men. "They're moving the toteboard," he said. "Yes," I said. They had dug the thing out of the ground and were moving it further west. Well, it put men to work. I liked to see men working. I had an idea that the security man was talking to me to find out if I was crazy or not. He probably wasn't. But I got the idea. I let ideas jump me like that. I scratched my belly and pretended that I was a good old guy. "They're going to put the lakes back in," I said. "Yeah," he said. "This place used to be called the Track of the Lakes and Flowers." "Is that so?" he said. "Yeah," I told him, "they used to have a Goose Girl contest. They'd choose a goose girl and she went out in a boat and rowed around among the geese. Real boring job." "Yeah," said the cop. He just stood there. I stood up. "Well," I said, "I'm going to get a coffee. Take it easy." "Sure," he said, "pick some winners."

"You too, man," I said. Then I walked away.

A title. My mind was blank. It was getting chilly. Being an old fart, I thought it might be best to get my jacket. I took the escalator down from the 4th floor. Who invented the escalator? Moving steps. Now, talk about crazy. People going up and down escalators, elevators, driving cars, having garage doors that open at the touch of a button. Then they go to health clubs to work the fat off. In 4,000 years we won't have any legs, we'll wiggle along on our assholes, or maybe we'll just roll along like tumbleweeds. Each species destroys itself. What killed the dinosaurs was that they ate everything around and then had to eat each other and that brought it down to one and the son-of-a-bitch just starved to death.

I got down to my car, got my jacket, put it on, took the escalator back up. That made me feel more like a playboy, a hustler—leaving the place and then coming back. I felt as if I had consulted some special secret source.

Well, I played out the card, had some luck. By the 13th race it was dark and beginning to rain. I bet ten minutes early and left. Traffic was cautious. Rain scares the hell out of L.A. drivers. I got on the freeway behind the mass of red taillights. I didn't turn on the radio. I wanted silence. A title ran through my brain: *Bible for the Disenchanted*. No, no good. I remembered some of the best titles. I mean, of other writers. *Bow Down to Wood and Stone*. Great title, lousy writer. *Notes from the Underground*. Great title. Great writer. Also, *The Heart Is a Lonely Hunter*. Carson McCullers, a very underrated writer. Of all my dozens of titles the one I liked best was *Confessions of a Man Insane Enough to Live with Beasts*. But I blew that one away on a little mimeo pamphlet. Too bad.

Then the freeway stopped and I just sat there. No title. My head was empty. I felt like sleeping for a week. I was glad I had put the trash cans out. I was tired. Now I didn't have to do it. Trash cans. One night I had slept, drunk, on top of trash cans. New York City. I was awakened by a big rat sitting on my belly. We both, at once, leaped about 3 feet into the air. I was trying to be a writer. Now I was supposed to be one and I couldn't think of a title. I was a fake. Traffic began to move and I followed it along. Nobody knew who anybody else was and it was great. Then a great flash of lightning crashed above the freeway and for the first time that day I felt pretty good.

So, after some days of blank-braining it, I awakened this morning and there was the title, it had come to me in my sleep: *The Last Night of the Earth Poems*. It fit the content, poems of finality, sickness and death. Mixed with others, of course. Even some humor. But the title works for this book and this time. Once you get a title, it locks everything in, the poems find their order. And I like the title. If I saw a book with a title like that I would pick it up and try to read a few pages. Some titles exaggerate to attract attention. They don't work because the lie doesn't work.

Well, I'm done with that. Now what? Back to the novel and more poems. Whatever happened to the short story? It has left me. There's a reason but I don't know what it is. If I worked at it I could find the reason but working at it wouldn't help anything. I mean, that time could be used for the novel or the poem. Or to cut my toenails.

You know, somebody ought to invent a decent toenail clipper. I'm sure it can be done. The ones they give us to work with are really awkward and disheartening. I read where a guy on skid row tried to hold up a liquor store with a pair of toenail clippers. It didn't work there either. How did Dostoevsky cut his toenails? Van Gogh? Beethoven? Did they? I don't believe it. I used to let Linda do mine. She did an excellent job—only now and then she got a little piece of flesh. Me, I've had enough pain. Of any kind.

I know that I'm going to die soon and it seems very strange to me. I'm selfish, I'd just like to keep my ass writing more words. It puts the glow in me, tosses me through golden air. But really, how much longer can I go on? It's not right to keep going on. Hell, death is the gasoline in the tank anyhow. We need it. I need it. You need it. We trash up the place if we stay too long.

Strangest thing, I think, after people die is looking at their shoes. That's the saddest thing. It's as if most of their personality remains in their shoes. The clothes, no. It's in the shoes. Or a hat. Or a pair of gloves. You take a person who has just died. You put their hat, their gloves and their shoes on the bed and look at them and you'll go crazy. Don't do it. Anyhow, now they know something that you don't. Maybe.

Last day of racing today. I played inter-track wagering, at Hollywood Park, betting Fairplex Park. Bet all 13 races. Had a lucky day. Came out totally refreshed and strong. Wasn't even bored out there today. Felt jaunty, in touch. When you're up, it's great. You notice things. Like driving back, you notice the steering wheel on your car. The instrument panel. You feel like you're in a god-damned space ship. You weave in and out of traffic, neatly, not rudely—working distances and speeds. Stupid stuff. But not today. You're up and you stay up. How odd. But you don't fight it. Because you know it won't last. Off day tomorrow. Oaktree Meet, Oct. 2. The meets go around and around, thousands of horses running. As sensible as the tides, a part of them.

Even caught the cop car tailing me on the Harbor Freeway south. In time. I slowed it to 60. Suddenly, he dropped way back. I held it at 60. He'd almost clocked me at 75. They hate Acuras. I stayed at 60. For 5 minutes. He roared past me doing a good 90. Bye, bye, friend. I hate getting a ticket like anybody else. You have to keep using the rear view mirror. It's simple. But you're bound to get tagged finally. And when you do, be glad you're not drunk or packing drugs. If you're not. Anyhow, the title's in.

And now I'm up here with the Macintosh and there is a wondrous space before me. Terrible music on the radio but you can't expect a 100 percent day. If you get 51, you've won. Today was a 97.

I see where Mailer has written a huge new novel about the CIA and etc. Norman is a professional writer. He asked my wife once, "Hank doesn't like my writing, does he?" Norman, few writers like other writers' works. The only time they like them is when they are dead or if they have been dead for a long time. Writers only like to sniff their own turds. I am one of those. I don't even like to talk to writers, look at them or worse, listen to them. And the worst is to drink with them, they slobber all over themselves, really look piteous, look like they are searching for the wing of the mother.

I'd rather think about death than about writers. Far more pleasant.

I'm going to turn this radio off. The composers also sometimes screw it up. If I had to talk to somebody I think I'd much prefer a computer repairman or a mortician. With or without drinking. Preferably with.

Death comes to those who wait and to those who don't. Burning day today, burning dumb day. Came out of the post office and my car wouldn't kick over. Well, I am a decent citizen. I belong to the Auto Club. So, I needed a telephone. Forty years ago telephones were everywhere. Telephones and clocks. You could always look somewhere and see what time it was. No more. No more free time. And public telephones are vanishing.

I went by instinct. I went into the post office, took a stairway down and there in a dark corner, all alone and unannounced was a telephone. A sticky dirty dark telephone. There was not another within two miles. I knew how to work a telephone. Maybe. Information. The operator's voice came through and I felt saved. It was a calm and boring voice and asked me what city I wanted. I named the city and the Auto Club. (You have to know how to do all the little things and you have to do them over and over again or you are dead. Dead in the streets. Unattended, unwanted.) The lady gave me a number but it was a wrong number. For the business office. Then I got the garage. A macho voice, cool, weary yet combative. Wonderful. I gave him the info. "30 minutes," he said.

I went back to the car, opened a letter. It was a poem. Christ. It was about me. And him. We had met, it seemed, twice, about 15 years ago. He had also published me in his magazine. I was a great poet, he said, but I drank. And had lived a miserable down-and-out life. Now young poets were drinking and living miserable and down-and-out

35

lives because they thought that was the way to make it. Also, I had attacked other people in my poems, including him. And I had imagined that he had written unflattering poems about me. Not true. He was really a nice person, he said he had published many other poets in his magazine for 15 years. And I was not a nice person. I was a great writer but not a nice person. And he never would have ever "paled" around with me. That's what he wrote: "paled." And he kept spelling "you're" as "your." He wasn't a good speller.

It was hot in the car. It was 100 degrees, the hottest Oct. first since 1906.

I wasn't going to respond to his letter. He would write again.

Another letter from an agent, enclosing the work of a writer. I glanced. Bad stuff. Of course. "If you have any suggestions on his writing or any publishing leads, we would much appreciate …"

Another letter from a lady thanking me for sending her husband a few lines and a drawing at her suggestion, that it made him very happy. But now they were divorced and she was freelancing it and could she come by and interview me?

Twice a week I get requests for interviews. There's just not that much to talk about. There are plenty of things to write about but not to talk about.

I remember once, in the old days, some German journalist was interviewing me. I had poured wine into him and had talked for 4 hours. After that, he had leaned forward drunkenly and said, "I am no interviewer. I just wanted an excuse to see you …"

I tossed the mail to the side and sat waiting. Then I saw the tow truck. A young smiling fellow. Nice boy. Sure.

"HEY, BABY!" I yelled, "OVER HERE!"

He backed it around and I got out and told him the problem.

"Tow me into the Acura garage," I told him.

"Your warranty still good on that car?" he asked.

He knew damn well it wasn't. It was 1991 and I was driving a 1989.

"Doesn't matter," I said, "tow me to the Acura dealer."

"Take them a long time to fix it, maybe a week."

"Hell no, they are very fast."

"Listen," said the boy, "we have our own garage. We can take it down there, maybe fix it today. If not, we'll write you up and give you a call at first opportunity."

Right there I visualized my car at their garage for a week. To be told that I needed a new camshaft. Or my cylinder heads ground.

"Tow me to Acura," I said.

"Wait," said the boy, "I gotta call my boss first."

I waited. He came back.

"He said to jump start you."

"What?"

"Jump start."

"All right, let's do it."

I got in my car and let it roll to the back of his truck. He got out the snakes and it started right up. I signed the papers and he drove off and I drove off....

Then I decided to drop the car off at the corner garage.

"We know you. You been coming here for years," said the manager.

"Good," I said, then smiled, "so don't screw me."

He just looked at me.

"Give us 45 minutes."

"All right."

"You need a ride?"

"Sure."

He pointed. "He'll take you."

Nice boy standing there. We walked to his car. I gave him the directions. We drove up the hill.

"You still making movies?" he asked me.

I was a celebrity, you see.

"No," I said, "fuck Hollywood."

He didn't understand that.

"Stop here," I said.

"Oh, that's a big house."

"I just work there," I said.

It was true.

I got out. Gave him 2 dollars. He protested but took them.

I walked up the driveway. The cats were sprawled about, pooped. In my next life I want to be a cat. To sleep 20 hours a day and wait to be fed. To sit around licking my ass. Humans are too miserable and angry and single-minded.

I walked up and sat at the computer. It's my new consoler. My writing has doubled in power and output since I have gotten it. It's a magic thing. I sit in front of it like most people sit in front of their tv sets.

"It's only a glorified typewriter," my son-in-law told me once.

But he isn't a writer. He doesn't know what it is when words bite into space, flash into light, when the thoughts that come into the head can be followed at once by words, which encourages more thoughts and more words to follow. With a typewriter it's like walking through mud. With a computer, it's ice skating. It's a blazing blast. Of course, if there's nothing inside you, it doesn't matter. And then there's the clean-up work, the corrections. Hell, I used to have to write everything twice. The first time to get it down and the second time to correct the errors and fuckups. This way, it's one run for the fun, the glory and the escape.

I wonder what the next step will be after the computer? You'll probably just press your fingers to your temples and out will come this mass of perfect wordage. Of course, you'll have to fill up before you start but there will always be some lucky ones who can do that. Let's hope.

The phone rang.

"It's the battery," he said, "you needed a new battery."

"Suppose I can't pay?"

"Then we'll hold your spare tire."

"Be down soon."

And as soon as I started down the hill I heard my elderly neighbor. He was yelling at me. I climbed his steps. He was dressed in his pajama pants and an old gray sweatshirt. I walked up and shook his hand.

"Who are you?" he asked.

"I'm your neighbor. Been there for ten years."

"I'm 96," he said.

"I know it, Charley."

"God won't take me because He's afraid I'll take his job."

"You could."

"Could take the Devil's job too."

"You could."

"How old are *you*?"

"71."

"71?"

"Yes."

"That's old too."

"Oh, I know it, Charley."

We shook hands and I went back down his steps and then on down the hill, passing the tired plants, the tired houses.

I was on my way to the gas station.

Just another day kicked in the ass.

Today was the second day of inter-track wagering. Where the live horses ran at Oak Tree there were only 7,000 people. Many people don't want to make that long drive to Arcadia. For those living in the south part of town, it means taking the Harbor Freeway, then the Pasadena Freeway and then after that more driving along surface streets to get to the track. It's a long hot drive, coming and going. I always came in from that drive total-ly exhausted.

A small-time trainer phoned me. "There was nobody out there. It's the end. I need a new trade. Think I'll get a word processor and become a writer. I'll write about you…"

His voice was on the message machine. I phoned him back and congratulated him for coming in 2nd on a 6-to-1 shot. But he was down.

"The small trainer is finished. This is the end," he said.

Well, we'll see what they draw tomorrow. Friday. Probably a thousand more. It's not only inter-track wager-ing, it's the economy. Things are worse than the govern-ment or the press will admit. Those who are still alive in the economy are keeping quiet about it. I'd have to guess that the biggest business going is the sale of drugs. Hell, take that away and almost all the young would be unem-ployed. Me, I'm still making it as a writer but that could be shot through the head overnight. Well, I still have my old age pension: $943.00 a month. They gave me that

41

when I turned 70. But that can die too. Imagine all the old wandering the streets without their pensions. Don't discount it. The national debt can pull us under like a giant octopus. People will be sleeping in the graveyards. At the same time, there is a crust of living rich on top of the rot. Isn't it astonishing? Some people have so damn much money they don't even know how much they have. And I'm talking millions. And look at Hollywood, turning out 60 million dollar movies, as idiotic as the poor fools who go to see them. The rich are still there, they've always found a way to milk the system.

I remember when the racetracks were jammed with people, shoulder to shoulder, ass to ass, sweating, screaming, pushing toward the full bars. It was a good time. Have a big day, you'd find a lady at the bar and that night in your apartment you'd both be drinking and laughing. We thought those days (and nights) would never end. And why should they? Crap games in the parking lots. Fist fights. Bravado and glory. Electricity. Hell, life was good, life was funny. All us guys were men, we'd take no shit from anybody. And, frankly, it felt good. Booze and a roll in the hay. And plenty of bars, full bars. No tv sets. You talked and got into trouble. If you got picked up for being drunk in the streets they only locked you up overnight to dry out. You lost jobs and found other jobs. No use hanging around the same place. What a time. What a life. Crazy things always happening, followed by more crazy things.

Now, it has simmered away. Seven thousand people at a major racetrack on a sunny afternoon. Nobody at the bar. Just the lonely barkeep holding a towel. Where are the people? There are more people than ever but where are they? Standing on a corner, sitting in a room. Bush might get reelected because he won an easy war. But he didn't do crap for the economy. You never even know if your bank will open in the morning. I don't mean to sing the blues. But you know, in the 1930's at least everybody knew where they were. Now, it's a game of mirrors. And nobody is quite sure what is holding it together. Or who they are really working for. If they are working.

Damn, I've got to get off this. Nobody else seems to be bitching about the state of affairs. Or, if they are, they are in a place where nobody can hear them.

And I sit around writing poems, a novel. I can't help it, I can't do anything else.

I was poor for 60 years. Now I am neither rich nor poor.

At the track they are going to start laying off people at the concession stands, the parking lots and in the business office and in maintenance. Purses for races will decline. Smaller fields. Less jocks. A lot less laughter. Capitalism has survived communism. Now, it eats away at itself. Moving toward 2,000 A.D. I'll be dead and out of here. Leaving my little stack of books. Seven thousand at the track. Seven thousand. I can't believe it. The Sierra Madres weep in the smog. When the horses no longer run the sky will fall down, flat, wide, ponderous, crushing everything. Glassware won the 9th, paid $9.00. I had a ten on it.

Computer class was a kick for sore balls. You pick it up inch by inch and try to get the totality. The problem is that the books say one way and some people say the other. The terminology slowly becomes understandable. The computer only *does,* it doesn't *know.* You can confuse it and it can turn on you. It's up to you to get along with it. Still, the computer can go crazy and do odd and strange things. It catches viruses, gets shorts, bombs out, etc. Somehow, tonight, I feel that the less said about the computer, the better.

I wonder whatever happened to that crazy French reporter who interviewed me in Paris so long ago? The one who drank whiskey the way most men drink beer? And he got brighter and more interesting as the bottles emptied. Probably dead. I used to drink 15 hours a day but it was mostly beer and wine. I ought to be dead. I will be dead. Not bad, thinking about that. I've had a weird and woolly existence, much of it awful, total drudgery. But I think it was the *way* I rammed myself through the shit that made the difference. Looking back now, I think I exhibited a certain amount of cool and class no matter what was happening. I remember how the FBI guys got pissed driving me along in that car. "HEY, THIS GUY'S PRETTY COOL!" one of them yelled angrily. I hadn't asked what I had been picked up for or where we were going. It just didn't matter to me. Just another slice out of the senselessness of life. "NOW WAIT," I told them. "I'm scared." That seemed to make them feel better. To me, they were like creatures from outer space. We couldn't relate to each other. But it was strange. I felt nothing. Well, it wasn't exactly strange to me, I mean it was strange in the ordinary sense. I just saw hands and feet and heads. They had their minds made up about something, it was up to them. I wasn't looking for justice and logic. I never have. Maybe that's why I never wrote any social protest stuff. To me, the whole structure would never make sense no matter what they did with it. You really can't make something good out of something that isn't there. Those guys wanted me to show fear, they were used to that. I was just disgusted.

Now here I am going to a computer class. But it's all for the better, to play with words, my only toy. Just musing here tonight. The classical music on the radio is not too good. I think I'll shut down and go sit with the wife and cats for a while. Never push, never force the word. Hell, there's no contest and certainly very little competition. Very little.

Of course, there are some strange types at the race-track. There's one fellow who's out there almost every day. He never seems to win a race. After each race he screams in dismay about the horse that won. "IT'S A PIECE OF SHIT!" he will scream. And then go on shouting about how the horse never should have won. A good 5 minutes worth. Often the horse will read 5 to 2 and 3 to 1, 7 to 2. Now a horse like that must show something or the odds would be much higher. But to this gentleman it just doesn't make sense. And don't let him lose a photo finish. He really comes on with it then. "FUCK GOD IN THE FACE! HE CAN'T DO THIS TO ME!" I have no idea why he isn't barred from the track.

I asked another fellow once, "Listen, how does this guy make it?" I'd seen him talking to him at times.

"He borrows money," he told me.

"But doesn't he run out of lenders?"

"He finds new ones. You know his favorite expression?"

"No."

"When does the bank open in the morning?"

I guess he just wants to be at the track, somehow, just to be there. It means something to him even if he continues to lose. It's a place to be. A mad dream. But it's boring there. A groggy place. Everybody thinking that they alone know the angle. Dumb lost egos. I'm one of those. Only it's a hobby for me. I think. I hope. But there is something there, if only in a short time frame, very short,

47

a flash, like when my horse is in the run and then it does it. I see it happening. There is a high, a lift. Life becomes almost sensible when the horses do your bidding. But the spaces in between are very flat. People standing about. Most of them losers. They begin to look dry as dust. They are sucked dry. Yet, you know, when I force myself to stay home I begin to feel very listless, sick, useless. It's strange. The nights are always all right, I type at night. But the days have to be gotten rid of. I'm sick too in a way. I am not facing reality. But who the hell wants to?

It reminds me of when I stayed in this Philadelphia bar from 5 a.m. until 2 a.m. It seemed the only place I could be. Often I didn't even remember going to my room and coming back. I seemed always on that bar stool. I was evading the realities, I didn't like them.

Maybe for this fellow the racetrack was like the bar was for me?

All right, you tell me something useful. Be a lawyer? A doctor? A congressman? That's crap too. They think it isn't crap but it is. They are locked into a system and they can't get out. And almost everybody is not very good at what they do. It doesn't matter, they are in the safe cocoon.

It got kind of funny out there one day. I'm speaking of the racetrack again.

The Crazy Screamer was there as usual. But there was another fellow, you could see that there was something wrong with his eyes. They looked angry. He was standing near the Screamer and listening. Then he listened to the Screamer's predictions for the next race. The Screamer was good that way. And evidently Angry Eyes was betting the Screamer's tips.

The day wore on. I was coming out of the men's room and then I saw and heard it. Angry Eyes was yelling at the Screamer, *"God-damn you, shut up! I'm going to kill you!"* The Screamer turned his back and walked off saying, "Please ... Please ..." in a very weary and disgusted manner. Angry Eyes followed him: "YOU SON-OF-A-BITCH! I'M GOING TO KILL YOU!"

Security arrived and intercepted Angry Eyes and led him off. Evidently death at the racetrack was not to be condoned.

Poor Screamer. He was quiet the remainder of the day. But he stayed the full card. Gambling, of course, can eat you alive.

I had a girlfriend once who said, "You're really in bad shape, you go to both Alcoholics Anonymous and Gamblers Anonymous at the same time." But she really didn't mind either of those things unless they interfered with bed exercises. Then she hated them.

I remember a friend of mine who was a total gambler. He told me once, "I don't care if I win or lose, I just want to gamble."

I'm not that way, I've been on Starvation Row too many times. Not having any money at all only has the slightest tinge of Romanticism when you are very young.

Anyway, the Screamer was out there again the next day. Same thing: he railed against the results of each race. He's a genius in a way because he never picks a winner. Think of this. It's a very hard thing to do. I mean, even if you know nothing, you can just take a number, any number, say 3. You can bet 3 for 2 or 3 days and you are bound to finally get a winner. But not this fellow. He is a marvel. He knows all about horses, fractional times, track variants, pace, class, etc. but he still manages only to pick losers. Think of it. Then forget it or it will drive you crazy.

I picked up $275 today. I started playing the horses late, when I was 35. I've been at them for 36 years and I figure they still owe me $5,000. Should the gods allow me 8 or 9 more years I might die even.

Now that's a goal worth shooting for, don't you think? Huh?

Burned out. A couple nights of drinking this week. Got to admit I don't recover as fast as I used to. Best thing about being tired is that you don't come out (in the writing) with any wild and dizzy proclamations. Not that that is bad unless it becomes habitual. The first thing writing should do is save your own ass. If it does this, then it will be automatically juicy, entertaining.

Writer I know is phoning people telling them that he types 5 hours a night. I imagine that we are supposed to marvel at this. Of course, do I have to tell you? What matters is *what* he is typing. I wonder if he counts his telephone time as part of his 5 hours of typing?

I can type from one to 4 hours but the 4th hour, somehow, tapers away into almost nothing. Knew a guy once who told me, "We fucked all night." It's not the same fellow who types 5 hours a night. But they've met each other. Maybe they ought to take turns, switch off. The guy who typed 5 hours gets to fuck all night and the guy who fucked all night gets to type 5 hours. Or maybe they can fuck each other while somebody else types. Not me, please. Have the woman do it. If there is one ...

Hmmm ... you know, I am feeling somewhat goofy tonight. I keep thinking of Maxim Gorky. Why? I don't know. Somehow it seems as if Gorky never really existed. Some writers you can believe were there. Like Turgenev or D. H. Lawrence. Hemingway appears to me to be half-and-half. He was really there but he wasn't. But Gorky? He did write some strong things. Before the Revolution.

53

Then after the Revolution his writing began to pale. He didn't have much to bitch about. It's like the anti-war protesters, they need a war in order to thrive. There are some who make good livings protesting against war. And when there isn't a war they don't know what to do. Like during the Gulf War there was a group of writers, poets, they had planned a huge anti-war protest, they were ready with their poems and speeches. Suddenly the war was over. And the protest was scheduled for a week later. But they didn't call it off. They went ahead with it anyway. Because they wanted to be on stage. They needed it. It was something like an Indian doing a Rain Dance. I myself am anti-war. I was anti-war long ago when it wasn't even a popular, decent and intellectual thing. But I am suspect of the courage and motivations of many of the professional anti-war protesters. From Gorky to this, what? Let the mind roll, who cares?

Another good day at the track. Don't worry, I'm not winning all the money. I usually bet $10 or $20 to win or when it really looks good to me, I'll go $40.

The racetracks further confuse the people. They have 2 fellows on tv before each race and they talk about who they think will win. They show a net loss on each meet. As do all the public handicappers, tout sheets and race betting services. Even computers can't figure the nags no matter how much info is fed into them. Any time you pay somebody to tell you what to do you are going to be a loser. And this includes your psychiatrist, your psychologist, your broker, your workshop teacher and your etc.

There is nothing that teaches you more than regrouping after failure and moving on. Yet most people are stricken with fear. They fear failure so much that they fail. They are too conditioned, too used to being told what to do. It begins with the family, runs through school and goes into the business world.

You see here, I have a couple of good days at the track and suddenly I know everything.

There is a door open into the night and I am sitting here freezing but I won't get up and close the door because these words are running away with me and I like that too much to stop. But, damn it, I will. I'll get up and close the door and take a piss.

There, I did it. Both of those things. I even put on a sweater. Old writer puts on sweater, sits down, leers into computer screen and writes about life. How holy can we get? And Christ, did you ever wonder how much piss a man pisses in a lifetime? How much he eats, shits? Tons. Horrible. It's best we die and get out of here, we are poisoning everything with what we expel. Damn the dancing girls, they do it too.

No horses tomorrow. Tuesday is an off day.

I think I'll go downstairs and sit with my wife, look at some dumb tv. I'm either at the track or at this machine. Maybe she's glad of it. I hope so. Well, here I go. I'm a good guy, you know? Down the stairs. It must be strange living with me. It's strange to me.

Good night.

This is one of those nights where there is nothing. Imagine being always like this. Scooped-out. Listless. No light. No dance. Not even any disgust.

This way, one doesn't even have the good sense to commit suicide. The thought doesn't occur.

Get up. Scratch yourself. Drink some water.

I feel like a mongrel dog in July, only it's October.

Still, I've had a good year. Masses of pages sit in the bookcase behind me. Written since Jan. 18. It's like a madman was turned loose. No sane man would write that many pages. It's a sickness.

This year has also been good because I've held back on visitors, more than ever before. I was tricked once though. Some man wrote me from London, said he had taught in Soweto. And when he had read his students some Bukowski many of them had shown a real interest. Black African kids. I liked that. I always like happenings from a distance. Later on this man wrote me that he worked for the *Guardian* and that he'd like to come by and interview me. He asked for my phone number, via mail, and I gave it to him. He phoned me. Sounded all right. We set a date and time and he was on his way. The night and time arrived and there he was. Linda and I set him up with wine and he began. The interview seemed all right, only a little off-hand, odd. He would ask a question, I would answer it and he would begin talking about some experience he had had, relating more or less to the question and the answer I had given. The wine kept pouring and the

57

interview was over. We drank on and he talked about Africa, etc. His accent began changing, altering, getting, I think, grosser. And he seemed to be getting more and more stupid. He was metamorphosing right in front of us. He got onto sex and stayed there. He liked black girls. I said that we didn't know many, but that Linda had a friend who was a Mexican girl. That did it. He began on how much he liked Mexican girls. He had to meet this Mexican girl. It was a must. We said, well, we didn't know. He kept on and on. We were drinking good wine but his mind acted as if it had been blasted by whiskey. Soon it just got down to "Mexican ... Mexican ... where is this Mexican girl?" He had dissolved completely. He was just a sloppy senseless barroom drunk. I told him that the night was over. I had to make the track the next day. We moved him toward the door. "Mexican, Mexican...," he said.

"You will send us a copy of the interview, yes?" I asked.

"Of course, of course," he said. "Mexican ..."

We closed the door and he was gone.

Then we had to drink to rid him from our minds.

That was months ago. No article ever arrived. He had nothing to do with the *Guardian*. I don't know if he really phoned from London. He was probably phoning from Long Beach. People use the ruse of the interview to get in the door. And since there is usually no payment for an interview, anybody can up and knock on the door with a tape recorder and a list of questions. A fellow with a German accent came by one night with his recorder. He made claim to belonging to some German publication

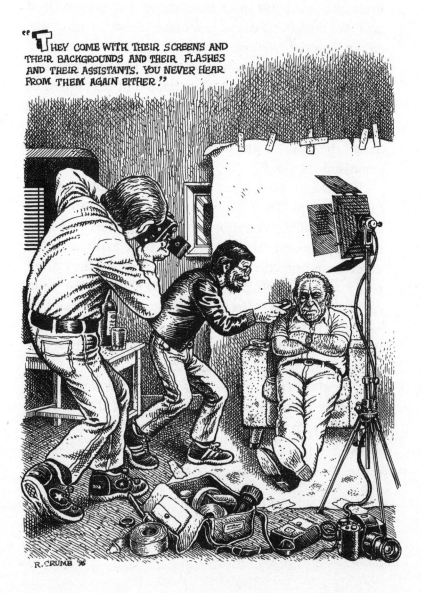

that had a circulation of millions. He stayed for hours. His questions seemed dumb but I opened up, tried to make it lively and good. He must have gotten 3 hours worth of tape. We drank and drank and drank. Soon his head was falling forward. We drank him under the table and were ready to go further. Really have a ball. His head bent forward on his chest. Little driblets ran out of the corners of his mouth. I shook him. "Hey! Hey! Wake up!" He came around and looked at me. "I have got to tell you something," he said, "I am no interviewer, I just wanted to come and see you."

There have been times when I was a sucker for photographers too. They claim connections, send samples of their work. They come by with their screens and their backgrounds and their flashes and their assistants. You never hear from them again either. I mean, they never send back any photographs. Not any. They are the greatest liars. "I'll send you a complete set." One man said, "I am going to send you one that will be full size." "What do you mean?" I asked. "I'm going to send you a 7 by 4 foot photo." That was a couple of years ago.

I've always said, a writer's job is to write. If I get burned by these fakes and sons-of-bitches, it's my fault. I'm done with them all. Let them toady up to Elizabeth Taylor.

The dangerous life. Had to get up at 8 a.m. to feed the cats because the Westec Security man was coming by at 8:30 a.m. to begin the installation of a more sophisticated warning system. (Am I the one who used to sleep on top of garbage cans?)

Westec Security arrived at exactly 8:30 a.m. A good sign. I took him around the house pointing out windows, doors, etc. Good, good. We would wire them, we would install glass-breaking detectors, low beams, cross beams, fire sprinklers, etc. Linda came down and asked some questions. She is better at that than I.

I had one thought: "How long will this take?"

"Three days," he said.

"Jesus Christ," I said. (Two of those days the race-track would be closed.)

So we fumbled around and left him in there, told him we'd be back soon. We had a $100 gift certificate at I. Magnin's somebody had given us for our wedding anniversary. Also, I had a royalty check to deposit. So, off to the bank. I signed the check.

"I really like your signature," the girl said.

Another girl walked over and looked at the signature.

"His signature keeps changing," said Linda.

"I have to keep signing my name in books," I said.

"He's a writer," Linda said.

"Really? What do you write?" one of the girls asked.

"Tell her," I said to Linda.

"He writes poems, short stories and novels," she said.

"And a screenplay," I said. "*Barfly.*"

"Oh," smiled one of the girls, "I saw it."

"Did you like it?"

"Yes," she smiled.

"Thank you," I said.

Then we turned and walked off.

"I heard one of the girls say as we walked in, 'I know who that is,' " said Linda.

See? We were famous. We got into the car and drove over to the shopping center to get something to eat near I. Magnin's.

We got a table, had turkey sandwiches, apple juice and cappuccinos. From the table we could see a goodly portion of the mall. The place was virtually empty. Business was bad. Well, we had a hundred dollar coupon to blow. We'd help the economy.

I was the only man there. Just women sat at the tables, alone, or in twos. The men were elsewhere. I didn't mind. I felt safe with the ladies. I was resting. My wounds were healing. I could stand a little shade. Damned if I could leap off of cliffs forever. Maybe after a respite I could dive over the edge again. Maybe.

We finished eating and went over to I. Magnin's.

I needed shirts. I looked at shirts. Couldn't find a damned one. They looked like they had been designed by half-wits. I passed. Linda needed a purse. She found one, marked down 50%. It was $395. It just didn't look like $395. More like $49.50. She passed. There were 2 chairs with elephant heads on the backs. Nice. But they were thousands. There was a glass bird, nice, $75 but Linda said we had no place to put it. Same with the fish with blue stripes. I was getting tired. Looking at things made me tired. Department stores wore me down and stamped on me. There was nothing in them. Tons and tons of crap. If it were free, I wouldn't take it. Don't they ever sell anything likeable?

. We decided maybe another day. We went to a bookstore. I needed a book on my computer. I needed to know more. Found a book. Went to the clerk. He tabbed it up. I paid with a card. "Thank you," he said, "would you be good enough to sign this?" He handed me my latest book. There, I was famous. Noticed twice in the same day. Twice was enough. Three times or more and you were in trouble. The gods were making it just right for me. I asked his name, wrote it in, scribbled something, my name and a drawing.

We stopped at the computer store on the way in. I needed paper for the laser printer. They didn't have any. I showed my fist to the clerk. Made me think of the old days. He recommended a place. We found it on the way in. We found everything there, cut-rate. I got enough laser paper to last two years and likewise mailing envelopes, pens, paper clips. Now, all I had to do was write.

We drove on in. The security man had left. The tile man had come and gone. He left a note, "I will be back by 4 p.m." We knew the tile man wouldn't be back at 4 p.m. He was crazy. Bad childhood. Very confused. But good with tiles.

I packed the stuff upstairs. I was ready. I was famous. I was a writer.

I sat down and opened the computer. I opened it to STUPID GAMES. Then I started playing *Tao*. I was getting better and better at it. I seldom lost to the computer. It was easier than beating the horses but somehow not as fulfilling. Well, I'd be back Wednesday. Playing the horses tightened up my screws. It was part of the scheme. It worked. And I had 5,000 sheets of laser paper to fill.

Terrible day at the track, not so much in money lost, I may even have won a bob, but the feeling out there was horrible. Nothing was stirring. It was as if I was doing time and you know, I don't have much time left. The same faces, the same 18 percent take. Sometimes I feel as if we are all trapped in a movie. We know our lines, where to walk, how to act, only there is no camera. Yet, we can't break out of the movie. And it's a bad one. I know each of the mutuel clerks all too well. We sometimes have small conversations as I bet. It's my wish to find a noncommittal clerk, one who will simply punch out my tickets and say nothing. But, they all get social, finally. They are bored. And they are on guard too: many of the horseplayers are somewhat deranged. There are often confrontations with the clerks, loud buzzers sound and security comes running. By talking to us, the clerks can feel us out. They feel safer that way. They prefer the friendly bettor.

The horseplayers are easier for me. The regulars know that I am some kind of nut and don't wish to speak to them. I am always working on a new system, often changing systems in midstream. I am always trying to fit numbers around actuality, trying to code the madness into a simple number or a group of numbers. I want to understand life, happenings in life. I read an article wherein it was stated that for some long period of time now, in chess, a king, a bishop and a rook were believed to be equal to a king and two knights. A Los Alamos machine with 65,536 processors was put to work on the program. The computer solved the problem in 5 hours after considering 100 billion moves by working backwards from the winning position. It was found that the king, the rook and the bishop could defeat the king and two knights in 223 moves. This is utterly fascinating to me. It certainly beats the ponderous, tiddlywinks game of betting on the horses.

I believe that I worked too long in my life as a common laborer. I worked as such until I was 50 years old. Those bastards got me used to going somewhere every day and staying somewhere for many hours and then returning. I feel guilty just lolling about. So, I find myself at the track, bored and, at the same time, going crazy. I reserve the nights for the computer or for drinking or for both. Some of my readers think I love horses, that the action excites me, that I am a gung-ho gambler, a real macho big time boy. I get books in the mail about horses and horse racing and stories about the track and etc. I don't give a damn about that stuff. I go to the track almost reluctantly. I am too idiotic to figure out any other place to go. Where, where, during the day? The Hanging Gardens? A motion picture? Hell, help me, I can't sit around with the ladies and most men my age are dead and if they aren't dead they should be because they surely seem to be.

I've tried staying away from the track but then I get very nervous and depressed and that night there are absolutely no juices to lend the computer. I guess getting my ass out of here forces me to look at Humanity and when you look at Humanity you've GOT to react. It's all too much, a continuous horror show. Yeah, I'm bored out there, I'm terrorized out there but I'm also, so far, some kind of student. A student of hell.

Who knows? Some day soon I might be bedridden. I'll lay there and paint on sheets of paper tacked to the wall. I'll paint them with a long brush and probably even like it.

But right now, it's the faces of the horseplayers, card-board faces, horrible, evil, blank, greedy, dying faces, day after day. Tearing up their tickets, reading their various papers, watching the changes on the toteboard as they are being ground away to less and less, as I stand there with them, as I am one with them. We are sick, the suckerfish of hope. Our poor clothing, our old cars. We move toward the mirage, our lives wasted like everybody else's.

Stayed home from the track today, have had a sore throat and a pain at the top of my head, a little toward the right side of it. When you get to be 71 you can never tell when your head is going to explode through the windshield. I still go after a good drunk now and then, and smoke far too many cigarettes. The body gets pissed off at me for doing this, but the mind must be fed too. And the spirit. Drinking feeds my mind and my spirit. Anyhow, I stayed in from the track, slept until 12:20 p.m.

Easy day. Got in the spa like a big timer. The sun was out and the water bubbled and whirled, hot. I soothed out. Why not? Get an edge. Try to feel better. The whole world is a sack of shit ripping open. I can't save it. But I've gotten many letters from people who claim that my writing has saved their asses. But I didn't write it for that, I wrote it to save my own ass. I was always outside, never fit. I found that out in the schoolyards. And another thing I learned was that I learned very slowly. The other guys knew everything; I didn't know a fucking thing. Everything was bathed in a white and dizzying light. I was a fool. And yet, even when I was a fool I knew that I wasn't a complete fool. I had some little corner of me that I was protecting, there was something there. No matter. Here I was in a spa and my life was closing down. I didn't mind, I had seen the circus. Still, there are always more things to write until they throw me into the darkness or into whatever it is. That's the good thing about the word, it just keeps trotting on, looking for things, forming sentences, having a ball. I was full of words and they still came out in good form. I was lucky. In the spa. Bad throat, pain in head, I was lucky. Old writer in spa, musing. Nice, nice. But hell is always there, waiting to unfurl.

My old yellow cat came up and looked at me in the water. We looked at each other. We each knew everything and nothing. Then he walked off.

The day went on. Linda and I had lunch somewhere, don't remember where. Food not so good, packed with Saturday people. They were alive but they weren't alive. Sitting at the tables and booths, eating and talking. Wait, Jesus, that reminds me. Had lunch the other day before going to the track. Sat at the counter, it was completely empty. I had gotten my order and was eating. Man walked in and took the seat RIGHT NEXT TO MINE. There were 20 or 25 other seats. He took the one next to me. I'm just not that fond of people. The further I am from them the better I feel. And he put in his order and started talking to the waitress. About professional football. I watch it sometimes myself, but to talk about it in a cafe? They went on and on, dribbles about this and that. On and on. Favorite player. Who should win, etc. Then somebody at a booth joined in. I suppose I wouldn't have minded it all so much if I hadn't been rubbing elbows with that bastard next to me. A good sort, sure. He liked football. Safe. American. Sitting next to me. Forget it.

So yes, we had lunch, Linda and I, got back and it went restfully toward the night, then just after dark Linda noticed something. She was good at that sort of thing. I saw her coming back through the yard and she said, "Old Charley fell, the fire department is there."

70

Old Charley is the 96-year-old guy who lives in the big house next door to us. His wife died last week. They were married 47 years.

I walked out front and there was the fire truck. There was a fellow standing there. "I'm Charley's neighbor. Is he alive?"

"Yes," he said.

It was evident that they were waiting for the ambulance. The fire truck had gotten there first. Linda and I waited. The ambulance came. It was odd. Two little guys got out, they seemed quite small. They stood side by side. Three fire engine guys surrounded them. One of them started talking to the little guys. They stood there and nodded. Then that was over. They walked around and got the stretcher. They carried it up the long stairway to the house.

They were in there a very long time. Then out they came. Old Charley was strapped onto the stretcher. As they got ready to load him into the ambulance we stepped forward. "Hold on, Charley," I said. "We'll be waiting for you to come back," Linda said.

"Who are you?" Charley asked.

"We're your neighbors," Linda answered.

Then he was loaded in and gone. A red car followed with 2 relatives in it.

My neighbor walked over from across the street. We shook hands. We'd been on a couple of drunks together. We told him about Charley. And we were all miffed that the relatives left him alone so much. But there wasn't much we could do.

"You oughta see my waterfall," said my neighbor.

"All right," I said, "let's see it."

We walked over there, through his wife, past his kids and out the back door and into the backyard past his pool and sure enough there in the back was a HUGE waterfall. It went all the way up a cliff in the back and some of the water seemed to be coming out of a tree trunk. It was massive. And built of huge and beautiful stones of different colors. The water roared down flooded by lights. It was hard to believe. There was a worker back there still working on the waterfall. There was more to be done on it.

I shook hands with the worker.

"He's read all your books," my neighbor said.

"No shit," I said.

The worker smiled at me.

Then we walked back into the house. My neighbor asked me, "How about a glass of wine?"

I told him, "No, thanks." Then explained the sore throat and the pain at the top of my head.

Linda and I walked back across the street and back to our place.

And, basically, that was about the day and the night.

Well, my 71st year has been a hell of a productive year. I have probably written more words this year than in any year of my life. And though a writer is a poor judge of his own work, I still tend to believe that the writing is about as good as ever—I mean, as good as I have done in my peak times. This computer that I started using on Jan. 18 has had much to do with it. It's simply easier to get the word down, it transfers more quickly from the brain (or wherever this comes from) to the fingers and from the fingers to the screen where it is immediately visible—crisp and clear. It's not a matter of speed per se, it's a matter of flow, a river of words and if the words are good then let them run with ease. No more carbons, no more retyping. I used to need one night to do the work and then the next night to correct the errors and sloppiness of the night before. Misspellings, screw-ups in tenses, etc. can now all be corrected on the original copy without a complete retype or write-ins or cross-outs. Nobody likes to read haphazard copy, not even the writer. I know all this must sound prissy and over-careful but it isn't, all it does is allow whatever force or luck you might have engendered to come out clearly. It's all for the best, really, and if this is how you lose your soul, I am all for it.

There have been some bad moments. I remember one night after typing a good 4 hours or so, I felt I had had some astonishing luck when—I hit something or other—there was a flash of blue light and the many pages of writing vanished. I tried everything to get them back. They were simply gone. Yes, I had it set on "Save-all," it still didn't matter. This had happened at other times but not with so many pages. Let me tell you, it is one hell of a hell of a horrible feeling when the pages vanish. Come to think of it now, I have lost 3 or 4 pages at other times on my novel. A whole chapter. What I did then was simply rewrite the whole damn thing. When you do this, you lose something, little highlights that don't return but you gain something too because as you rewrite you skip some parts that didn't quite please you and you add some parts that are better. So? Well, it's a long night then. The birds are up. The wife and the cats think you've gone mad.

I consulted some computer experts about the "blue flash" but none of them could tell me anything. I've found out that most computer experts aren't very expert. Confounding things happen that just aren't in the book. Now that I know more about computers I think I know one thing that might have brought the work back from the "blue flash"...

The worst night was when I sat down to the computer and it went completely crazy, sending out bombs, weird loud sounds, moments of darkness, deathly blackness, I worked and worked but could do nothing. Then I noticed what looked like liquid that had hardened on the screen and around the slot near the "brain," the slot where you inserted the disks. One of my cats had sprayed the machine. I had to take it down to the computer shop. The mechanic was out and a salesman removed a portion of the "brain," a yellow liquid splashed on his white shirt and he screamed "cat spray!" Poor guy. Poor guy. Anyhow, I left the computer. Nothing in the warranty covered cat spray. They had to take practically all the guts out of the "brain." It took them 8 days to fix it. During that time I went back to my typewriter. It was like trying to break rock with my hands. I had to learn to type all over again. I had to get good and drunk to get the flow. And again, it was one night to write it and another night to straighten it out. But I was glad the typer was there. We had been together over 5 decades and had some great times. When I got the computer back it was with some sadness that I returned the old typer to its place in the corner. But I went back to the computer and the words flew like crazy birds. And there were no longer any blue flashes and pages that vanished. Things were even better. That cat spraying the machine fixed everything up. Only now, when I leave the computer I cover it with a large beach towel and close the door.

Yes, it's been my most productive year. Wine gets better if it's properly aged.

I'm not in a contest with anybody, have no thoughts about immortality, don't give a damn about it. It's the ACTION while you're alive. The gate springing open in the sunlight, the horses plunging through the light, all the jocks, brave little devils in their bright silks, going for it, doing it. The glory is in the motion and the dare. Death be damned. It's today and today and today. Yes.

The tide ebbs. I sit and stare at a paper clip for 5 minutes. Yesterday, coming in on the freeway, it was evening going into darkness. There was a light fog. Christmas was coming like a harpoon. Suddenly I noticed that I was driving almost alone. Then in the road I saw a large bumper attached to a piece of grill. I avoided it in time, then looked to my right. There was a pile-up of cars, 4 or 5 cars but there was silence, no movement, nobody around, no fire, no smoke, no headlights. I was going too fast to see if there were people in the cars. Then, at once, evening became night. Sometimes there is no warning. Things occur in seconds. Everything changes. You're alive. You're dead. And things move on.

We are paper thin. We exist on luck amid the percentages, temporarily. And that's the best part and the worst part, the temporal factor. And there's nothing you can do about it. You can sit on top of a mountain and meditate for decades and it's not going to alter. You can alter yourself into acceptability but maybe that's wrong too. Maybe we think too much. Feel more, think less.

All the cars in that pile-up seemed to be gray. Odd.

I like the way philosophers break down the concepts and theories which have preceded them. It's been going on for centuries. No, that's not the way, they say. This is the way. It goes on and on and seems very sensible, this onwardness. The main problem for the philosophers is that they must humanize their language, make it more accessible, then the thoughts light up better, are more

77

interesting still. I think that they are learning this. Simplicity is the key.

In writing you must slide along. The words can be crippled and choppy but if they slide along then a certain delight lights up everything. Careful writing is deathly writing. I think Sherwood Anderson was one of the best at playing with words as if they were rocks, or bits of food to be eaten. He PAINTED his words on paper. And they were so simple that you felt rushes of light, doors opening, walls glistening. You could see rugs and shoes and fingers. He had the words. Delightful. Yet, they were like bullets too. They could take you right out. Sherwood Anderson knew something, he had the instinct. Hemingway tried too hard. You could feel the hard work in his writing. They were hard blocks stuck together. And Anderson could laugh while he was telling you something serious. Hemingway could never laugh. Anybody who writes standing up at 6 a.m. in the morning has no sense of humor. He wants to defeat something.

Tired tonight. Damn, I don't get enough sleep. I would love to sleep until noon but with the first post at 12:30, add the drive and getting your figures ready, I have to leave here about 11 a.m., before the mailman gets here. And I'm seldom asleep until 2 a.m. or so. Get up a couple of times to piss. One of the cats awakens me at 6 a.m. on the dot, morning after morning, he's got to go out. Then too, the lonelyhearts like to phone before 10 a.m. I don't answer, the machine takes the message. I mean, my sleep is broken. But if this is all I have to bitch about then I'm in grand shape.

No horses for the next 2 days. I won't be up until noon

tomorrow and I'll feel like a powerhouse, ten years younger. Hell, that's to laugh—ten years younger would make me 61, you call that a break? Let me cry, let me cry.

It's 1 a.m. Why don't I stop now and get some sleep?

Well, I move back and forth between the novel and the poem and the racetrack and I'm still alive. There isn't much going on at the track, I'm just stuck with humanity and there I am. Then there's the freeway, to get there and back. The freeway always reminds you of what most people are. It's a competitive society. They want you to lose so they can win. It's inbred and much of it comes out on the freeway. The slow drivers want to block you, the fast drivers want to get around you. I hold it at 70 so I pass and am passed. The fast drivers I don't mind. I get out of their way and let them go. It's the slow ones who are the irritants, those who do 55 in the fast lane. And sometimes you can get boxed in. And you see enough of the head and the neck of the driver ahead of you to take a reading. The reading is that this person is asleep at the soul and at the same time embittered, gross, cruel and stupid.

I hear a voice now saying to me, "You are stupid to think like that. You are the stupid one."

There are always those who will defend the subnormals in society because they don't realize the subnormals are subnormal. And the reason they don't realize it is that they too are subnormal. We have a subnormal society and that's why they act as they do and do to each other what they do. But that's their business and I don't mind it except that I have to live with them.

I recall once having dinner with a group of people. At a nearby table there was another group of people. They talked loudly and kept laughing. But their laughter was utterly false, forced. It went on and on.

Finally I said to the people at our table, "It's pretty bad, isn't it?"

One of the people at our table turned to me, put on a sweet smile and said, "I like it when people are happy."

I didn't respond. But I felt a dark black hole welling in my gut. Well, hell.

You get a reading on people on the freeways. You get a reading on people at dinner tables. You get a reading on people on tv. You get a reading on people in the supermarket, etc., etc. It's the same reading. What can you do? Duck and hold on. Pour another drink. I like it when people are happy too. I just haven't seen very many.

So, I got to the track today and took my seat. There was a guy wearing a red cap backwards. One of those caps that the tracks give away. Giveaway Day. He had his Racing Form and a harmonica. He picked up the harmonica and blew. He didn't know how to play it. He just blew. And it wasn't Schoenberg's 12 tone scale either. It was a 2 or 3 tone scale. He ran out of wind and picked up his Racing Form.

In front of me sat the same 3 guys who were there all week. A guy of about 60 who always wore brown clothes and a brown hat. Next to him sat another older guy, about 65, his hair very white, snow white with a crooked neck and round shoulders. Next to him was an oriental about 45 who kept smoking cigarettes. Before each race they discussed which horse they were going to bet. These were amazing bettors, much like the Crazy Screamer I told you about before. I'll tell you why. I have sat behind them for two weeks now. And none of them has yet picked a winner. And they bet the short odds too, I mean between 2 to 1 and 7 or 8 to 1. That's maybe 45 races times 3 selections. That's 135 selections without a winner. This is a truly amazing statistic. Think about it. Say if each of them just picked a number like 1 or 2 or 3 and stayed with it they would automatically pick a winner. But by jumping around they somehow managed, using all their brain power and know-how, to keep on missing. Why do they keep coming to the racetrack? Aren't they ashamed of their ineptness? No, there is always the next race. Someday they will hit. Big.

You must understand then, when I come from the track and off of the freeway, why this computer looks so good to me? A clean screen to lay words on. My wife and my 9 cats seem like the geniuses of the world. They are.

What do writers do when they aren't writing? Me, I go
to the racetrack. Or in the early days, I starved or worked
at gut-wrenching jobs.

I stay away from writers now—or people who call
themselves writers. But from 1970 until about 1975
when I just decided to sit in one place and write or die,
writers came by, all of them poets. POETS. And I discovered a curious thing: none of them had any visible
means of support. If they had books out they didn't sell.
And if they gave poetry readings, few attended, say from
4 to 14 other POETS. But they all lived in fairly nice
apartments and seemed to have plenty of time to sit on
my couch and drink my beer. I had gotten the reputation
in town of being the wild one, of having parties where
untold things happened and crazy women danced and
broke things, or I threw people off my porch or there
were police raids or etc. and etc. Much of this was true.
But I also had to get the word down for my publisher and
for the magazines to get the rent and the booze money,
and this meant writing prose. But these ... poets ... only
wrote poetry ... I thought it was thin and pretentious
stuff ... but they went on with it, dressed themselves in a
fairly nice manner, seemed well-fed, and they had all this
couch-sitting time and time to talk—about their poetry
and themselves. I often asked, "Listen, tell me, how do
you make it?" They just sat there and smiled at me and
drank my beer and waited for some of my crazy women
to arrive, hoping that they might somehow get some of

it—sex, admiration, adventure or what the hell.

It was getting clear in my mind then that I would have to get rid of these soft toadies. And gradually, I found out their secret, one by one. Most often in the background, well hidden, was the MOTHER. The mother took care of these geniuses, got the rent and the food and the clothing.

I remember once, on a rare sojourn from my place, I was sitting in this POET's apartment. It was quite dull, nothing to drink. He sat speaking of how unfair it was that he wasn't more widely recognized. The editors, everybody was conspiring against him. He pointed his finger at me: "You too, you told Martin not to publish me!" It wasn't true. Then he went to bitching and babbling about other things. Then the phone rang. He picked it up and spoke very guardedly and quietly. He hung up and turned to me.

"It's my mother, she's coming over. You have to leave!"

"It's all right, I'd like to meet your mother."

"No! No! She's horrible! You have to leave! Now! Hurry!"

I took the elevator down and out. And wrote that one off.

There was another one. His mother bought him his food, his car, his insurance, his rent and even wrote some of his stuff. Unbelievable. And it had gone on for decades.

There was another fellow, he always seemed very calm, well-fed. He taught a poetry workshop at a church every Sunday afternoon. He had a nice apartment. He was a member of the communist party. Let's call him Fred. I asked an older lady who attended his workshop

"HE POINTED HIS FINGER AT ME: 'YOU TOO, YOU TOLD MARTIN NOT TO PUBLISH ME!' IT WASN'T TRUE. THEN HE WENT TO BITCHING AND BABBLING ABOUT OTHER THINGS."

R. CRUMB '96

and admired him greatly, "Listen, how does Fred make it?" "Oh," she said, "Fred doesn't want anybody to know because he's very private that way but he makes his money by scrubbing food trucks."

"Food trucks?"

"Yes, you know those wagons that go about dispensing coffee and sandwiches at break time and lunch time at work places, well, Fred scrubs those food trucks."

A couple of years went by and then it was discovered that Fred also owned a couple of apartment houses and that he lived mainly off the rents. When I found this out I got drunk one night and drove over to Fred's apartment. It was located over a little theater. Very arty stuff. I jumped out of my car and rang the bell. He wouldn't answer. I knew he was up there. I had seen his shadow moving behind the curtains. I went back to my car and started honking my horn and yelling, "Hey, Fred, come on out!" I threw a beer bottle at one of his windows. It bounced off. That got him. He came out on his little balcony and peered down at me. "Bukowski, go away!"

"Fred, come on down here and I'll kick your ass, you communist land owner!"

He ran back inside. I stood there and waited for him. Nothing. Then I got the idea that he was calling the police. I had seen enough of them. I got into my car and drove back to my place.

Another poet lived in this house down by the waterfront. Nice house. He never had a job. I kept after him, "How do you make it? How do you make it?" Finally, he gave in. "My parents own property and I collect the rents for them. They pay me a salary." He got a damned good salary, I imagine. Anyhow, at least *he* told me.

Some never do. There was this other guy. He wrote fair poetry but very little of it. He always had his nice apartment. Or he was going off to Hawaii or somewhere. He was one of the most relaxed of them all. Always in new and freshly pressed clothing, new shoes. Never needed a shave, a haircut; had bright flashing teeth. "Come on, baby, how do you make it?" He never let on. He didn't even smile. He just stood there silently.

Then there's another type that lives on handouts. I wrote a poem about one of them but never sent it out because I finally felt sorry for him. Here is some of it jammed together:

Jack with the hair hanging, Jack demanding money, Jack of the big gut, Jack of the loud, loud voice, Jack of the trade, Jack who prances before the ladies, Jack who thinks he's a genius, Jack who pukes, Jack who badmouths the lucky, Jack getting older and older, Jack still demanding money, Jack sliding down the beanstalk, Jack who talks about it but doesn't do it, Jack who gets away with murder, Jack who jacks, Jack who talks of the old days, Jack who talks and talks, Jack with the hand out, Jack who terrorizes the weak, Jack the embittered, Jack of the coffee shops, Jack screaming for recognition, Jack who never has a job, Jack who totally overrates his potential, Jack who keeps screaming about his unrecognized talent, Jack who blames everybody else.

You know who Jack is, you saw him yesterday, you'll see him tomorrow, you'll see him next week.

Wanting it without doing it, wanting it free.

Wanting fame, wanting women, wanting everything.

A world full of Jacks sliding down the beanstalk.

Now I'm tired of writing about poets. But I will add that they are hurting themselves by living as poets instead of as something else. I worked as a common laborer until I was 50. I was jammed in with the people. I never claimed to be a poet. Now I am not saying that working for a living is a grand thing. In most cases it is a horrible thing. And often you must fight to keep a horrible job because there are 25 guys standing behind you ready to take the same job. Of course, it's senseless, of course it flattens you out. But being in that mess, I think, taught me to lay off the bullshit when I did write. I think you have to get your face in the mud now and then, I think you have to know what a jail is, a hospital is. I think you have to know what it feels like to go without food for 4 or 5 days. I think that living with insane women is good for the backbone. I think you can write with joy and release after you've been in the vise. I only say this because all the poets I have met have been soft jellyfish, sycophants. They have nothing to write about except their selfish non-endurance.

Yes, I stay away from the POETS. Do you blame me?

I have no idea what causes it. It's just there: a certain feeling for writers of the past. And my feelings aren't even accurate, they are just mine, almost entirely invented. I think of Sherwood Anderson, for instance, as a little fellow, slightly slump-shouldered. He was probably straight and tall. No matter. I see him my way. (I've never seen a photo of him.) Dostoevsky I see as a bearded fellow on the heavy side with dark green smoldering eyes. First he was too heavy, then too thin, then too heavy. Nonsense, surely, but I like my nonsense. I even see Dostoevsky as a fellow who lusted for little girls. Faulkner, I see in a rather dim light as a crank and a fellow with bad breath. Gorky, I see as a sneak drunk. Tolstoy as a man who went into rages over nothing at all. I see Hemingway as a fellow who practiced ballet behind closed doors. I see Celine as a fellow who had problems sleeping. I see e. e. cummings as a great pool player. I could go on and on.

Mainly I had these visions when I was a starving writer, half-mad, and unable to fit into society. I had very little food but had much time. Whoever the writers were, they were magic to me. They opened doors differently. They needed a stiff drink upon awakening. Life was too god-damned much for them. Each day was like walking in wet concrete. I made them my heroes. I fed upon them. My ideas of them supported me in my nowhere. Thinking about them was much better than reading them. Like D. H. Lawrence. What a wicked little guy. He

91

knew so much that it just kept him pissed-off all the time. Lovely, lovely. And Aldous Huxley ... brain power to spare. He knew so much it gave him headaches.

I would stretch out on my starvation bed and think about these fellows.

Literature was so ... Romantic. Yeah.

But the composers and painters were good too, always going mad, suiciding, doing strange and obnoxious things. Suicide seemed such a good idea. I even tried it a few times myself, failed but came close, gave it some good tries. Now here I am almost 72 years old. My heroes are long past gone and I've had to live with others. Some of the new creators, some of the newly famous. They aren't the same to me. I look at them, listen to them and I think, is this all there is? I mean, they look comfortable ... they bitch ... but they look COMFORTABLE. There's no wildness. The only ones who seem wild are those who have failed as artists and believe that the failure is the fault of outside forces. And they create badly, horribly.

I have nobody to focus on anymore. I can't even focus on myself. I used to be in and out of jails, I used to break down doors, smash windows, drink 29 days a month. Now I sit in front of this computer with the radio on, listening to classical music. I'm not even drinking tonight. I am pacing myself. For what? Do I want to live to be 80, 90? I don't mind dying ... but not this year, all right?

I don't know, it just was different back then. The writers seemed more like ... writers. Things were done. The Black Sun Press. The Crosbys. And damned if once I didn't cross back into that age. Caresse Crosby published one of my stories in her *Portfolio* magazine along with Sartre, I think, and Henry Miller and I think, maybe, Camus. I don't have the mag now. People steal from me. They take my stuff when they drink with me. That's why more and more I am alone. Anyhow, somebody else must also miss the Roaring 20's and Gertrude Stein and Picasso ... James Joyce, Lawrence and the gang.

To me it seems that we're not getting through like we used to. It's like we've used up the options, it's like we can't do it anymore.

I sit here, light a cigarette, listen to the music. My health is good and I hope that I am writing as well or better than ever. But everything else I read seems so ... practiced ... it's like a well-learned style. Maybe I've read too much, maybe I've read too long. Also, after decades and decades of writing (and I've written a boat load) when I read another writer I believe I can tell exactly when he's faking, the lies jump out, the slick polish grates.... I can guess what the next line will be, the next paragraph.... There's no flash, no dash, no chance-taking. It's a job they've learned, like fixing a leaky faucet.

It was better for me when I could imagine greatness in others, even if it wasn't always there.

In my mind I saw Gorky in a Russian flophouse asking for tobacco from the fellow next to him. I saw Robinson Jeffers talking to a horse. I saw Faulkner staring at the last drink in the bottle. Of course, of course, it was foolish. Young is foolish and old is the fool.

I've had to adjust. But for all of us, even now, the next line is always there and it may be the line that finally breaks through, finally says it. We can sleep on that during the slow nights and hope for the best.

We're probably as good now as those bastards back then were. And some of the young are thinking of me as I thought of them. I know, I get letters. I read them and throw them away. These are the towering Nineties. There's the next line. And the line after that. Until there are no more.

Yeah. One more cigarette. Then I think I'll take a bath and go to sleep.

Bad day at the track. On the drive in, I always mull over which system I am going to use. I must have 6 or 7. And I certainly picked the wrong one. Still, I will never lose my ass and my mind at the track. I just don't bet that much. Years of poverty have made me wary. Even my winning days are hardly stupendous. Yet, I'd rather be right than wrong, especially when you give up hours of your life. One can feel time actually being murdered out there. Today, they were approaching the gate for the 2nd race. There were still 3 minutes to go and the horses and riders were slowly approaching. For some reason, it seemed an agonizingly long time for me. When you're in your 70's it hurts more to have somebody pissing on your time. Of course, I know, I had put myself into a position to be pissed upon.

I used to go to the night greyhound races in Arizona. Now, they knew what they were doing there. Just turn your back to get a drink and there was another race going off. No 30 minute waiting periods. Zip, zip, they ran them one after the other. It was refreshing. The night air was cold and the action was continuous. You didn't believe that somebody was trying to saw off your balls between races. And after it was all over, you weren't worn down. You could drink the remainder of the night and fight with your girlfriend.

But at the horse races it's hell. I stay isolated. I don't talk to anybody. That helps. Well, the mutuel clerks know me. I've got to go to the windows, use my voice.

Over the years, they get to know you. And most of them are fairly decent people. I think that their years of dealing with humanity has given them certain insights. For instance, they know that most of the human race is one large piece of crap. Still, I also keep my distance from the mutuel clerks. By keeping counsel with myself, I get an edge. I could stay home and do this. I could lock the door and fiddle with paints or something. But somehow, I've got to get out, and make sure that almost all humanity is still a large piece of crap. As if they would change! Hey, baby, I've got to be crazy. Yet there is something out there, I mean, I don't think about dying out there, for example, you feel too stupid being out there to be able to think. I've taken a notebook, thought, well, I'll write a few things between races. Impossible. The air is flat and heavy, we are all voluntary members of a concentration camp. When I get home, then I can muse about dying. Just a little. Not too much. I don't worry about dying or feel sorry about dying. It just seems like a lousy job. When? Next Wednesday night? Or when I'm asleep? Or because of the next horrible hangover? Traffic accident? It's a load, it's something that's got to be done. And I'm going out without the God-belief. That'll be good, I can face it head on. It's something you have to do like putting your shoes on in the morning. I think I'm going to miss writing. Writing is better than drinking. And writing while you're drinking, that's always made the walls dance. Maybe there's a hell, what? If there is I'll be there and you know what? All the poets will be there reading their works and I will have to listen. I will be drowned in their preening vanity, their overflowing self-esteem. If there is a hell, that will be my hell: poet after poet reading on and on....

Anyway, a particularly bad day. This system that usually worked didn't work. The gods shuffle the deck. Time is mutilated and you are a fool. But time is made to be wasted. What are you going to do about it? You can't always be roaring full steam. You stop and you go. You hit a high and then you fall into a black pit. Do you have a cat? Or cats? They sleep, baby. They can sleep 20 hours a day and they look beautiful. They know that there's nothing to get excited about. The next meal. And a little something to kill now and then. When I'm being torn by the forces, I just look at one or more of my cats. There are 9 of them. I just look at one of them sleeping or half-sleeping and I relax. Writing is also my cat. Writing lets me face it. It chills me out. For a while anyhow. Then my wires get crossed and I have to do it all over again. I can't understand writers who decide to stop writing. How do they chill out?

Well, the track was dull and deathly out there today but here I am back home and I'll be there tomorrow, most probably. How do I manage it?

Some of it is the power of routine, a power that holds most of us. A place to go, a thing to do. We are trained from the beginning. Move out, get into it. Maybe there's something interesting out there? What an ignorant dream. It's like when I used to pick up women in bars. I'd think, maybe *this* is the one. Another routine. Yet, even during the sex act, I'd think, this is another routine. I'm doing what I'm supposed to do. I felt ridiculous but I went ahead anyhow. What else could I do? Well, I should have

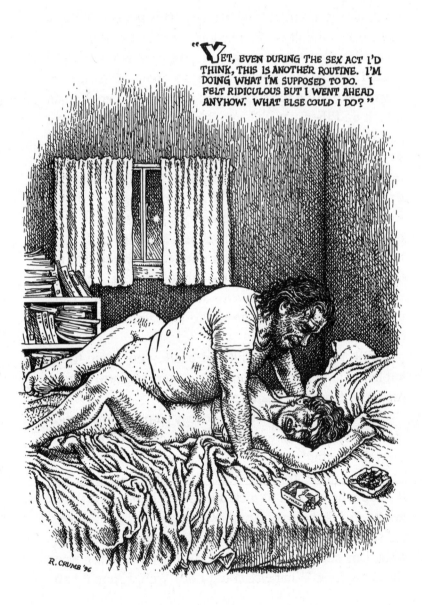

stopped. I should have crawled off and said, "Look, baby, we are being very foolish here. We are just tools of nature."

"What do you mean?"

"I mean, baby, you ever watched two flies fucking or something like that?"

"YOU'RE CRAZY! I'M GETTING OUT OF HERE!"

We can't examine ourselves too closely or we'll stop living, stop doing everything. Like the wise men who just sit on a rock and don't move. I don't know if that's so wise either. They discard the obvious but something *makes* them discard it. In a sense, they are one-fly-fucking. There's no escape, action or inaction. We just have to write ourselves off as a loss: any move on the board leads to a checkmate.

So, it was a bad day at the track today, I got a bad taste in the mouth of my soul. But I'll go tomorrow. I'm afraid not to. Because when I get back the words crawling across this computer screen really fascinate my weary ass. I leave it so that I can come back to it. Of course, of course. That's it. Isn't it?

I have probably written more and better in the past 2 years than at any time in my life. It's as if from over 5 decades of doing it, I might have gotten close to really doing it. Yet, in the past 2 months I have begun to feel a weariness. The weariness is mostly physical, yet it's also a touch spiritual. It could be that I am ready to go into decline. It's a horrible thought, of course. The ideal was to continue until the moment of my death, not to fade away. In 1989 I overcame TB. This year it has been an eye operation that has not as yet worked out. And a painful right leg, ankle, foot. Small things. Bits of skin cancer. Death nipping at my heels, letting me know. I'm an old fart, that's all. Well, I couldn't drink myself to death. I came close but I didn't. Now I deserve to live with what is left.

So, I haven't written for 3 nights. Should I go mad? Even at my lowest times I can feel the words bubbling inside of me, getting ready. I am not in a contest. I never wanted fame or money. I wanted to get the word down the way I wanted it, that's all. And I had to get the words down or be overcome by something worse than death. Words not as precious things but as necessary things.

Yet when I begin to doubt my ability to work the word I simply read another writer and then I know that I have nothing to worry about. My contest is only with myself: to do it right, with power and force and delight and gamble. Otherwise, forget it.

I have been wise enough to remain isolated. Visitors to this house are rare. My 9 cats run like mad when a human arrives. And my wife, too, is getting to be more and more like me. I don't want this for her. It's natural for me. But for Linda, no. I'm glad when she takes the car and goes off to some gathering. After all, I have my god-damned racetrack. I can always write about the racetrack, that great empty hole of nowhere. I go there to sacrifice myself, to mutilate the hours, to murder them. The hours must be killed. While you are waiting. The perfect hours are the ones at this machine. But you must have imperfect hours to get perfect hours. You must kill ten hours to make two hours live. What you must be careful of is not to kill ALL the hours, ALL the years.

You fix yourself up to be a writer by doing the instinctive things which feed you and the word, which protect you against death in life. For each, it's different. And for each, it changes. Once for me it meant very heavy drinking, drinking to the point of madness. It sharpened the word for me, brought it out. And I needed danger. I needed to put myself into dangerous situations. With men. With women. With automobiles. With gambling. With starvation. With anything. It fed the word. I had decades of that. Now it has changed. What I need now is more subtle, more invisible. It's a feeling in the air. Words spoken, words heard. Things seen. I still need a few drinks. But I am now into nuances and shadows. I am fed words by things that I am hardly aware of. This is good. I write a different kind of crap now. Some have noticed.

"You have broken through," is mainly what they tell me.

I am aware of what they sense. I feel it too. The words have gotten simpler yet warmer, darker. I am being fed from new sources. Being near death is energizing. I have all the advantages. I can see and feel things that are hidden from the young. I have gone from the power of youth to the power of age. There will be no decline. Uh uh. Now, pardon me, I must go to bed, it's 12:55 a.m. Talking the night off. Have your laugh while you can....

Well, I've been 72 years old for 8 days and nights now and I'll never be able to say that again.

It's been a bad couple of months. Weary. Physically and spiritually. Death means nothing. It's walking around with your ass dragging, it's when the words don't come flying from the machine, there's the gyp.

Now in my lower lip and under the lower lip, there is a large puffiness. And I have no energy. I didn't go to the track today. I just stayed in bed. Tired, tired. The Sunday crowds at the track are the worst. I have problems with the human face. I find it very difficult to look at. I find the sum total of each person's life written there and it is a horrible sight. When one sees thousands of faces in one day, it's tiring from the top of the head to the toes. And all through the gut. Sundays are so crowded. It's amateur day. They scream and curse. They rage. Then they go limp and leave, broke. What did they expect?

I had a cataract operation on my right eye a few months ago. The operation was not nearly as simple as the misinformation I gathered from people who claimed to have had eye operations. I heard my wife talking to her mother on the telephone: "You say it was over in a few minutes? And that you drove your car home afterwards?" Another old guy told me, "Oh, it's nothing, it's over in a flash and you just go about your business as normal." Others spoke about the operation in an off-hand manner. It was a walk in the park. Now, I didn't ask any of these people for information about the operation, they just came out with it. And after a while, I began to believe it. Although I still wondered how a thing as delicate as the eye could be treated more or less like cutting a toenail.

On my first visit to the doctor, he examined the eye and said that I needed an operation.

"O.k.," I said, "let's do it."

"What?" he asked.

"Let's do it now. Let's rock and roll!"

"Wait," he said, "first we must make an appointment with a hospital. Then there are other preparations. First, we want to show you a movie about the operation. It's only about 15 minutes long."

"The operation?"

"No, the movie."

What happens is that they take out the complete lens of the eye and replace it with an artificial lens. The lens is stitched in and the eye must adjust and recover. After about 3 weeks the stitches are removed. It's no walk in the park and the operation takes much longer than "a couple of minutes."

Anyhow, after it was all over, my wife's mother said it was probably an after-operational procedure she was thinking of. And the old guy? I asked him, "How long did it take for your sight to really get better after your eye operation?" "I'm not so sure I had an operation," he said.

Maybe I got this fat lip from drinking from the cat's water bowl?

I feel a little better tonight. Six days a week at the race-track can burn anybody out. Try it some time. Then come in and work on your novel.

Or maybe death is giving me some signs?

The other day I was thinking about the world without me. There is the world going on doing what it does. And I'm not there. Very odd. Think of the garbage truck coming by and picking up the garbage and I'm not there. Or the newspaper sits in the drive and I'm not there to pick it up. Impossible. And worse, some time after I'm dead, I'm going to be truly discovered. All those who were afraid of me or hated me when I was alive will suddenly embrace me. My words will be everywhere. Clubs and societies will be formed. It will be sickening. A movie will be made of my life. I will be made a much more courageous and talented man than I am. Much more. It will be enough to make the gods puke. The human race exaggerates everything: its heroes, its enemies, its importance.

The fuckers. There, I feel better. God-damned human race. There, I feel better.

The night is cooling off. Maybe I'll pay the gas bill. I remember in south central L.A. they shot a lady named Love for not paying her gas bill. The co. wanted to shut it off. She fought them off. Forget what with. Maybe a shovel. Cops came. Don't remember how it worked. Think she reached for something in her apron. They shot and killed her.

All right, all right, I'll pay the gas bill.

I worry about my novel. It's about a detective. But I keep getting him into these almost impossible situations and then I have to work him out. I sometimes think about how to get him out while I'm at the racetrack. And I know that my editor-publisher is curious. Maybe he thinks the work isn't literary. I say that anything I do is literary even if I try not to make it literary. He should trust me by now.

Well, if he doesn't want it, I'll unload it elsewhere. It will sell as well as anything I've written, not because it's better but because it's just as good and my crazy readers are ready for it.

Look, maybe a good night's sleep tonight and I'll wake up in the morning without this fat lip. Can you imagine me leaning toward the teller with this big lip and saying, "20 win on the 6 horse?" Sure. I know. He wouldn't even notice. My wife asked me, "Didn't you always have that?"

Jesus Christ.

Do you know that cats sleep 20 hours out of 24? No wonder they look better than I.

There are thousands of traps in life and most of us fall into many of them. The idea, though, is to stay out of as many of them as possible. Doing so helps you remain as alive as you might until you die....

The letter arrived from the offices of one of the network television stations. It was quite simple, stating that this fellow, let's call him Joe Singer, wants to come by. To talk about certain possibilities. On page 1 of the letter were stuck 2 one hundred dollar bills. On page 2 there was another hundred. I was on the way to the racetrack. I found that the hundred dollar bills peeled off of the pages nicely without damage. There was a phone number. I decided to call Joe Singer that night after the races.

Which I did. Joe was casual, easy. The idea, he said, was to create a series for tv based on a writer like myself. An old guy who was still writing, drinking, playing the horses.

"Why don't we get together and talk about it?" he asked.

"You'll have to come here," I said, "at night."

"O.k.," he said, "when?"

"Night after next."

"Fine. You know who I want to get to play you?"

"Who?"

He mentioned an actor, let's call him Harry Dane. I always liked Harry Dane.

"Great," I said, "and thanks for the 300."

"We wanted to get your attention."

"You did."

Well, the night came around and there was Joe Singer. He seemed likeable enough, intelligent, easy. We drank and talked, about horses and various things. Not much about the television series. Linda, my wife, was with us.

"But tell us more about the series," she said.

"It's all right, Linda," I said, "we're just relaxing ..."

I felt Joe Singer had more or less come by to see if I was crazy or not.

"All right," he said reaching into his briefcase, "here's a rough idea ..."

He handed me 4 or 5 sheets of paper. It was mostly a description of the main character and I thought they had gotten me down fairly well. The old writer lived with this young girl just out of college, she did all his dirty work, lined up his readings and stuff like that.

"The station wanted this young girl in there, you know," said Joe.

"Yeah," I said.

Linda didn't say anything.

"Well," said Joe, "you look this over again. There are also some ideas, plot ideas, each episode will have a different slant, you know, but it will all be based on your character."

"Yeah," I said. But I was beginning to get a bit apprehensive.

We drank another couple of hours. I don't remember

110

much about the conversation. Small talk. And the night ended....

The next day after the track I turned to the page about the episode ideas.

1. Hank's craving for a lobster dinner is thwarted by animal rights activists.

2. Secretary ruins Hank's chances with a poetry groupie.

3. To honor Hemingway, Hank bangs a broad named Millie whose husband, a jockey, wants to pay Hank to keep banging her. There must be a catch.

4. Hank allows a young male artist to paint his portrait and is painted into a corner into revealing his own homosexual experience.

5. A friend of Hank's wants him to invest in his latest scheme. An industrial use for recycled vomit.

I got Joe on the phone.

"Jesus, man, what's this about a homosexual experience? I haven't had any."

"Well, we don't have to use that one."

"Let's not. Listen, I'll talk to you later, Joe."

I hung up. Things were getting strange.

I phoned Harry Dane, the actor. He'd been over to the place two or three times. He had this great weather-

beaten face and he talked straight. He had few affecta-
tions. I liked him.

"Harry," I said, "there's this tv outfit, channel—they
want to do a series based on me and they want you to play
me. You heard from them?"

"No."

"I thought I might get you and this guy together and
see what happens."

"Channel what?"

I told him the channel.

"But that's commercial tv, censorship, commercials,
laugh tracks."

"This guy Joe Singer claims they have a lot of freedom
with what they can do."

"It's censorship, you can't offend the advertisers."

"What I like most is that he wanted you for the lead.
Why don't you come to my place and meet him?"

"I like your writing, Hank, if we could get, say, HBO
maybe we could do it right."

"Well, yeah. But why don't you come over, see what
he has to say? I haven't seen you for a while."

"That's right. Well, I'll come but it will be mainly to
see you and Linda."

"Fine. How about the night after next? I'll set it up."

"O.k.," he said.

I phoned Joe Singer.

"Joe. Night after next, 9 p.m. I've got Harry Dane
coming over."

"O.k., great. We can send a limo for him."

"Would he be alone in the limo?"

"Maybe. Or maybe some of our people would be in it."

"Well, I don't know. Let me call you back ..."

"Harry, they are trying to suck you in, they want to send a limo for you."

"Would it be just for me?"

"He wasn't quite sure."

"Can I have his phone number?"

"Sure."

And that was that.

When I came in after the track the next day Linda said, "Harry Dane phoned. We talked about the tv thing. He asked if we needed money. I told him we didn't."

"Is he still coming by?"

"Yes."

I came in a little early from the track the following day. I decided to hit the Jacuzzi. Linda was out, probably buying libations for the meeting. I, myself, was getting a little scared about the tv series. They could really fuck me over. Old writer does this. Old writer does that. Laugh track. Old writer gets drunk, misses poetry meeting. Well, that wouldn't be so bad. But I wouldn't want to write the crap, so the writing wouldn't be that good. Here I had written for decades in small rooms, sleeping on park benches, sitting in bars, working all the stupid jobs, meanwhile writing and writing exactly as I wanted to and felt I had to. My work was finally getting recognized. And I was still writing the way I wanted to and felt that I had to. I was still writing to keep from going crazy, I was still writing, trying to explain this god-damned life to myself. And here I was being talked into a tv series on commercial tv. All I had fought so hard for could be laughed right off the boards by some sitcom series with a laugh track. Jesus, Jesus.

I got undressed and stepped outside to the Jacuzzi. I was thinking about the tv series, my past life, now and everything else. I wasn't too aware. I stepped into the Jacuzzi at the wrong end.

I realized it the moment I stepped in. There weren't any steps at that end. It happened quickly. There was a small platform further in built to sit on. My right foot caught that, slipped off, and I was thrown off balance.

You're going to hit your head against the edge of the Jacuzzi, went through my mind.

I concentrated on pushing my head forward as I fell, letting all the rest go to hell. My right leg took the brunt of the fall, I twisted it but managed to keep my head from hitting the edge. Then I just floated in the bubbling water feeling the shots of pain in my right leg. I'd been having leg pains there anyhow, now it was really torn up. I felt foolish about it all. I could have knocked myself out. I could have drowned. Linda would have come back to find me floating and dead.

FAMOUS WRITER, FORMER SKID ROW POET
AND DRUNK FOUND DEAD IN HIS JACUZZI.

114

HE HAD JUST SIGNED A CONTRACT FOR A
SITCOM BASED UPON HIS LIFE.

That's not even an ignoble ending. That is just being
shit on entirely by the gods.

I managed to get out of the Jacuzzi and make my way
into the house. I could barely walk. Each step on the right
leg brought a mighty pain up the leg from the ankle to the
knee. I hobbled toward the refrigerator and pulled out a
beer....

Harry Dane arrived first. He had come in his own car.
We brought out the wine and I began pouring them. By
the time Joe Singer arrived, we'd had a few. I made the
introductions. Joe laid out the general format for the proposed series for Harry. Harry was smoking, and drinking
his wine pretty fast.

"Yeah, yeah," he said, "but a sound track? And Hank
and I would have to have total control over the material.
Then, I don't know. There's censorship ..."

"Censorship? What censorship?" asked Joe.

"Sponsors, you have to please the sponsors. There's a
limit on how far you can go with material."

"We'll have total freedom," said Joe.

"You can't have," said Harry.

"Laugh tracks are awful," said Linda.

"Yeah," I said.

"Then too," said Harry, "I've been in a tv series. It's a
drag, it takes hours and hours a day, it's worse than shooting a movie. It's hard work."

Joe didn't answer.

We all went on drinking. A couple of hours passed.

The same things seemed to be said over and over again. Harry saying maybe we should go to HBO. And that laugh tracks were awful. And Joe saying that everything would be all right, that there was plenty of freedom on commercial tv, that times had changed. It was really boring, really awful. Harry was really pouring down the wine. Then he got into what was wrong with the world and the main causes of it. He had a certain line he repeated quite often. It was a good line. Unfortunately, it was so good that I have forgotten it. But Harry went on.

All of a sudden Joe Singer leaped up. "Well, damn it, you guys have made a lot of lousy movies! Tv has done some good things! Everything we do isn't rotten! You guys keep on turning out crappy movies!"

Then he ran into the bathroom.

Harry looked at me and grinned. "Hey, he got mad, didn't he?"

"Yeah, Harry."

I poured some more wine. We sat and waited. Joe Singer stayed in the bathroom a long time. When he came out, Harry stood there talking to him. I couldn't hear what was being said. I think Harry felt sorry for him. It wasn't long after that, Singer started gathering his stuff into his briefcase. He walked to the door, then looked back at me, "I'll phone you," he said.

"O.k., Joe."

Then he was gone.

Linda, I and Harry kept on drinking. Harry went on with what was wrong with the world, repeating his good line which I can't remember. We didn't talk too much about the proposed tv series. When Harry left we worried about his driving. We said he could stay. He declined. He said he could make it. Luckily, he did.

Joe Singer phoned the next evening.

"Listen, we don't need that guy. He doesn't want to work. We can get somebody else."

"But, Joe, one of the main reasons I was interested at first was because of the possibility of Harry Dane."

"We can get somebody else. I'll write you, I'll send you a list, I'm going to work on it."

"I don't know, Joe ..."

"I'll write you. And listen, I talked to the people and they said, o.k., no laugh track. And they even said it would be o.k. to go to HBO. That surprised me because I work for them, I don't work for HBO. Anyhow, I'll send you a list of actors ..."

"All right, Joe ..."

I was still stuck in the web. Now I wanted out but I didn't quite know how to tell him. It surprised me, I was usually very good at getting rid of people. I felt guilty because he had probably put in a lot of work on the thing. And, originally, in the first flush of things, the idea of a series based mostly upon myself had probably appealed to my vanity. But now it didn't seem like a good thing. I felt crappy about the whole thing.

A couple of days later the photos of the actors arrived, a mass of them, and the preferred ones were circled. The agent's phone number was by each actor's photo. I was

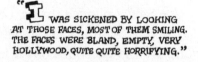

R. CRUMB '96

sickened by looking at those faces, most of them smiling. The faces were bland, empty, very Hollywood, quite quite horrifying.

Along with the photos was a short note:

"... going on a 3 week vacation. When I get back I am really going to kick this thing into gear ..."

The faces did it to me. I couldn't handle it any longer. I sat down and let go at the computer.

"... I've really been thinking about your project(s) and, frankly, I can't do it. It would mean the end of my life as I have lived it and have wanted to live it. It's just too big an intrusion into my existence. It would make me very unhappy, depressed. This feeling has been gradually coming over me but I just didn't quite know how to explain it to you. When you and Harry Dane had a falling out the other night, I felt great, I felt, now, it's over. But you bounce right back with a new list of actors. I want out, Joe, I can't handle it. I sensed it from the beginning and that sense grew stronger and stronger as things went along. Nothing against you, you are an intelligent young man who wants to pump some fresh blood into the tv scene—but let it not be mine. You may not understand my concern but, believe me, it's real, damned real. I should be honored that you want to display my life to the masses but, really, I am more than terrorized by the thought, I feel as if my very life were being threatened. I have to get out. I haven't been able to sleep nights, I haven't been able to think, I haven't been able to do anything.

Please, no phone calls, no letters. Nothing can change this.

The next day on the way to the racetrack I dropped the letter into the mailbox. I felt reborn. I might still have to fight some more to get free. But I'd go to court. Anything. Somehow, I felt sorry for Joe Singer. But, damn it all, I was free again.

On the freeway I turned on the radio and lucked onto some Mozart. Life could be good at times but sometimes some of that was up to us.

Was going down the escalator at the track after the 6th race when the waiter saw me. "You going home now?" he asked.

"I wouldn't do that to you, amigo," I told him.

The poor fellows had to bring the food from the track kitchen to the upper floors, carrying huge amounts on trays. When their clients ran out on them they had to pay the tab. Some of the players sat four to a table. The waiters could work all day and still owe the track money. And the crowded days were the worst, the waiters couldn't watch everybody. And when they did get paid the horseplayers tipped badly.

I went down to the first floor and stepped outside, stood in the sun. It was great out there. Maybe I'd just come to the track and stand in the sun. I seldom thought about writing out there but I did then. I thought about something that I had recently read, that I was probably the best selling poet in America and the most influential, the most copied. How strange. Well, to hell with that. All that counted was the next time I sat down to the computer. If I could still do it, I was alive; if I couldn't, everything that preceded meant little to me. But what was I doing, thinking about writing? I was cracking. I didn't even think about writing when I was writing. Then I heard the call to post, turned around, walked in and got back on the escalator. Going up, I passed a man who owed me money. He ducked his head down. I pretended not to see him. It didn't do any good after he'd paid me, he only borrowed it

back. An old guy had come up to me earlier that day: "Gimme 60 cents!" That gave him enough for a two buck bet, one more chance to dream. It was a sad god-damned place but almost every place was. There was no place to go. Well, there was, you could go to your room and close the door but then your wife got depressed. Or more depressed. America was the Land of Depressed Wives. And it was the fault of the men. Sure. Who else was around? You couldn't blame the birds, the dogs, the cats, the worms, the mice, the spiders, the fish, the etc. It was the men. And the men couldn't allow themselves to get depressed or else the whole ship would go down. Well, hell.

I was back at my table. Three men had the next table and they had a little boy with them. Each table had a small tv set, only theirs was turned on LOUD. The kid had it on some sitcom and that was nice of the men to let the kid look at his program. But he wasn't paying any attention to it, he wasn't listening, he was sitting there pushing around a rolled-up piece of paper. He bounced it against some cups, then he took it and tossed it into this cup and that. Some of the cups were filled with coffee. But the men just went on talking about the horses. My god, that tv was LOUD. I thought of saying something to the men, asking them to lower the tv a bit. But the men were black and they'd think I was racist. I left my table and walked out to the betting windows. I was unlucky, I got in a slow line. There was an old guy up front having trouble making his bets. He had his Form spread out across the window, along with his program and he was very hesitant about what he wanted to do. He probably lived in an old folks home or an institution of some sort but he was out for a day at the races. Well, no law against that and no law against him being in a fog. But somehow it hurt. Jesus, I don't have to suffer this, I thought. I had memorized the back of his head, his ears, his clothing, the bent back. The horses were nearing the gate. Everybody was screaming at him. He didn't notice them. Then, painfully, we watched as he slowly reached for his wallet. Slow, slow motion. He opened it and peered into it. Then he poked his fingers in there. I don't even want to go on. He finally paid and the clerk slowly handed him back his money. Then he stood there looking at his money and his tickets, then he turned back to the clerk and said, "No, I wanted the 6-4 exacta, not this ..." Somebody yelled out an obscenity. I walked off. The horses leaped out of the gate and I walked to the men's room to piss.

When I came back the waiter had my bill ready. I paid, tipped 20% and thanked him.

"See you tomorrow, amigo," he said.

"Maybe," I said.

"You'll be here," he said.

The other races ground on. I bet early on the 9th and left. I left ten minutes before post. I got to my car and moved out. At the end of parking on Century Boulevard by the signal there was an ambulance, a fire engine and two police cars. Two cars had hit head-on. There was glass everywhere, the cars were really mangled. Somebody had been in a hurry to get in and somebody had been in a hurry to get out. Horseplayers.

I moved around the crash and took a left on Century.

Just another day shot through the head and buried. It was a Saturday afternoon in hell. I drove along with the others.

Talk about a writer's block. I believe I was bitten by a spider. Three times. Noticed these 3 large red welts on my left arm the night of 9-08-92. Around 9 p.m. There was a slight pain to the touch. I decided to ignore it. But after 15 minutes I showed the marks to Linda. She had been to an emergency room earlier in the day. Something had left a stinger in her back. Now it was after 9 p.m., everything was closed except the Emergency Ward of the local hospital. I had been there before: I had fallen into a hot fireplace while drunk. I had not fallen into the fire directly but had fallen upon the hot surface while only wearing my shorts. Now, it was this. These welts.

"I think I'd feel like a fool going in there with just these welts. There are people in there bloodied from car crashes, knifings, shootings, attempted suicides, and all I have are 3 red welts."

"I don't want to wake up with a dead husband in the morning," Linda said.

I thought about it for 15 minutes, then said, "All right, let's go in."

It was quiet in there. The lady at the desk was on the telephone. She was on the telephone for some time. Then she was finished.

"Yes?" she asked.

"I think I've been bitten by something," I said. "Maybe I should be looked at."

127

I gave her my name. I was in the computer. Last visit: TB time.

I was walked into a room. The nurse did the usual. Blood pressure. Temperature.

Then the doctor. He examined the welts.

"Looks like a spider," he said, "they usually bite 3 times."

I was given a tetanus shot, a prescription for some antibiotics and some Benadryl.

We drove off to an all-night Sav-on to get the stuff.

The 500mg Duricef was to be taken one capsule every 12 hours. The Benadryl one every 4 to 6 hours.

I began. And this is the point. After a day or so I felt similar as I had to the time I had been taking antibiotics for TB. Only then, due to my weakened state, I was barely able to walk up and down the stairway, having to pull myself along by the banister. Now it was just the nauseous feeling, the dullness of the mind. Sick through the body, dull through the mind. About the 3rd day I sat down in front of this computer to see if anything would come out of it. I only sat there. This must be, I thought, the way it feels when it finally leaves you. And there is nothing you can do. At the age of 72 it was always possible that it would leave me. The ability to write. It was a fear. And it was not about fame. Or about money. It was about me. I was spoiled. I needed the outlet, the entertainment, the release of writing. The safety of writing. The damned job of it. All the past meant nothing. Reputation meant nothing. All that mattered was the next line. And if the next line wouldn't come, I was dead, even though, technically, I was living.

I have been off the antibiotics now for 24 hours but I still feel dull, a bit ill. The writing here lacks spark and gamble. Too bad, kid.

Now, tomorrow, I must see my regular doctor to find out if I need more antibiotics or what. The welts are still there, though smaller. Who knows what the hell?

Oh yes, the nice lady at the receptionist's desk, just as I was leaving, began talking about spider bites. "Yes, there was this fellow in his twenties. He got bit by a spider, now he's paralyzed from the waist up."

"Is that so?" I asked.

"Yes," she said, "and there was another case. This fellow ..."

"Never mind," I told her, "we have to leave."

"Well," she said, "have a nice night."

"You too," I said.

I feel poisoned tonight, pissed-on, used, worn to the nub. It's not entirely old age but it might have something to do with it. I think that the crowd, that crowd, Humanity which has always been difficult for me, that crowd is finally winning. I think the big problem is that it's all a repeat performance for them. There's no freshness in them. Not even the tiniest miracle. They just grind on and over me. If, one day, I could just see ONE person doing or saying something unusual it would help me get on with it. But they are stale, grimy. There's no lift. Eyes, ears, legs, voices but ... nothing. They congeal within themselves, kid themselves along, pretending to be alive.

It was better when I was young, I was still looking. I prowled the streets of night looking, looking ... mixing, fighting, searching ... I found nothing. But the total scene, the nothingness, hadn't quite taken hold. I never really found a friend. With women, there was hope with each new one but that was in the beginning. Even early on, I got it, I stopped looking for the Dream Girl; I just wanted one that wasn't a nightmare.

With people, all I found were the living who were now dead—in books, in classical music. But that helped, for a while. But there were only so many lively and magical books, then it stopped. Classical music was my stronghold. I heard most of it on the radio, still do. And I am ever surprised, even now, when I hear something strong and new and unheard before and it happens quite often. As I write this I am listening to something on the radio that I have never heard before. I feast on each note like a man starving for a new rush of blood and meaning and it's there. I am totally astonished by the mass of great music, centuries and centuries of it. It must be that many great souls once lived. I can't explain it but it is my great luck in life to have this, to sense this, to feed upon and celebrate it. I never write anything without the radio on to classical music, it has always been a part of my work, to hear this music as I write. Perhaps, some day, somebody will explain to me why so much of the energy of the Miracle is contained in classical music? I doubt that this will ever be told to me. I will only be left to wonder. Why, why, why aren't there more books with this power? What's wrong with the writers? Why are there so few good ones?

Rock music does not do it for me. I went to a rock concert, mainly for the sake of my wife, Linda. Sure, I'm a good guy, huh? Huh? Anyhow, the tickets were free, courtesy of the rock musician who reads my books. We were to be in a special section with the big shots. A director, former actor, made a trip to pick us up in his sport wagon. Another actor was with him. These are talented people, in their way, and not bad human beings. We drove to the director's place, there was his lady friend, we saw their baby and then off we all went in a limo. Drinks, talk. The concert was to be at Dodger Stadium. We arrived late. The rock group was on, blasting, enormous sound. 25,000 people. There was a vibrancy there but it was short-lived. It was fairly simplistic. I suppose the lyrics were all right if you could understand them. They were probably speaking of Causes, Decencies, Love found and lost, etc. People need that—anti-establishment, anti-parent, anti-something. But a successful millionaire group like that, no matter what they said, THEY WERE NOW ESTABLISHMENT.

Then, after a while, the leader said, "This concert is dedicated to Linda and Charles Bukowski!" 25,000 people cheered as if they knew who we were. It is to laugh.

The big shot movie stars milled about. I had met them before. I worried about that. I worried about directors and actors coming to our place. I disliked Hollywood, the movies seldom ever worked for me. What was I doing with these people? Was I being sucked in? 72 years of fighting the good fight, then to be sucked away?

The concert was almost over and we followed the director to the VIP bar. We were among the select. Wow!

There were tables in there, a bar. And the famous. I made for the bar. Drinks were free. There was a huge black bartender. I ordered my drink and told him, "After I drink this one, we'll go out back and duke it out."

The bartender smiled.

"Bukowski!"

"You know me?"

"I used to read your "Notes of a Dirty Old Man" in the *L.A. Free Press* and *Open City*."

"Well, I'll be god-damned ..."

We shook hands. The fight was off.

Linda and I talked to various people, about what I don't know. I kept going back to the bar again and again for my vodka 7's. The bartender poured me tall ones. I'd also loaded up in the limo on the way in. The night got

easier for me, it was only a matter of drinking them down big, fast and often.

When the rock star came in I was fairly far gone but still there. He sat down and we talked but I don't know about what. Then came black-out time. Evidently we left. I only know what I heard later. The limo got us back but as I reached the steps of the house I fell and cracked my head on the bricks. We had just had the bricks put in. The right side of my head was bloody and I had hurt my right hand and my back.

I found most of this out in the morning when I rose to take a piss. There was the mirror. I looked like the old days after the barroom fights. Christ. I washed some of the blood away, fed our 9 cats and went back to bed. Linda wasn't feeling too well either. But she had seen her rock show.

I knew I wouldn't be able to write for 3 or 4 days and that it would be a couple of days before I got back to the racetrack.

It was back to classical music for me. I was honored and all that. It's great that the rock stars read my work but I've heard from men in jails and madhouses who do too. I can't help it who reads my work. Forget it.

It's good sitting here tonight in this little room on the second floor listening to the radio, the old body, the old mind mending. I belong here, like this. Like this. Like this.

Went to the track today in the rain and watched 7 consensus favorites out of 9 win. There is no way I can make it when this occurs. I watched the hours get slugged in the head and looked at the people studying their tout sheets, newspapers and Racing Forms. Many of them left early, taking the escalators down and out. (Gunshots outside now as I write this, life back to normal.) After about 4 or 5 races I left the clubhouse and went down to the grandstand area. There was a difference. Fewer whites, of course, more poor, of course. Down there, I was a minority. I walked about and I could feel the desperation in the air. These were 2 dollar bettors. They didn't bet favorites. They bet the shots, the exactas, the daily doubles. They were looking for a lot of money for a little money and they were drowning. Drowning in the rain. It was grim there. I needed a new hobby.

The track had changed. Forty years ago there had been some joy out there, even among the losers. The bars had been packed. This was a different crowd, a different city, a different world. There was no money to blow to the sky, no to-hell-with-it money, no we'll-be-back-tomorrow money. This was the end of the world. Old clothing. Twisted and bitter faces. The rent money. The 5 dollars an hour money. The money of the unemployed, of the illegal immigrants. The money of the petty thieves, the burglars, the money of the disinherited. The air was dark. And the lines were long. They made the poor wait in long lines. The poor were used to long lines. And they stood in them to have their small dreams smashed.

This was Hollywood Park, located in the black district, in the district of Central Americans and other minorities.

I went back upstairs to the clubhouse, to the shorter lines. I got into line, bet 20 win on the second favorite.

"When ya gonna do it?" the clerk asked me.

"Do what?" I asked.

"Cash some tickets."

"Any day now," I told him.

I turned and walked away. I could hear him say something else. Old bent white haired guy. He was having a bad day. Many of the mutuel clerks bet. I tried to go to a different clerk each time I bet, I didn't want to fraternize. The fucker was out of line. It was none of his business if I ever cashed a bet. The clerks rode with you when you were running hot. They would ask each other, "What'd he bet?" But go cold on them, they got pissed. They should do their own thinking. Just because I was there every day didn't mean I was a professional gambler. I was a professional writer. Sometimes.

I was walking along and I saw this kid rushing toward me. I knew what it was. He blocked my path.

"Pardon me," he said, "are you Charles Bukowski?"

"Charles Darwin," I said, then stepped around him.

I didn't want to hear it, whatever he had to say.

I watched the race and my horse came in second, beaten out by another favorite. On off or muddy tracks too many favorites win. I don't know the reason but it occurs. I got the hell out of the racetrack and drove on in.

Got to the place, greeted Linda. Checked the mail.

Rejection letter from the *Oxford American*. I checked the poems. Not bad, good but not exceptional. Just a losing day. But I was still alive. It was almost the year 2,000 and I was still alive, whatever that meant.

We went out to eat at a Mexican place. Much talk about the fight that night. Chavez and Haugin before 130,000 in Mexico City. I didn't give Haugin a chance. He had guts but no punch, no movement and he was about 3 years past his prime. Chavez could name the round.

That night it was the way it was. Chavez didn't even sit down between rounds. He was hardly breathing heavily. The whole thing was a clean, sheer, brutal event. The body shots Chavez landed made me wince. It was like hitting a man in the ribs with a sledgehammer. Chavez finally got bored with carrying his man and took him out.

"Well, hell," I said to my wife, "we paid to see exactly what we thought we would see."

The tv was off.

Tomorrow the Japanese were coming by to interview me. One of my books was now in Japanese and another was on the way. What would I tell them? About the horses? About the strangling life in the darkness of the grandstand? Maybe they would just ask questions. They should. I was a writer, huh? How strange it was but everybody had to be something didn't they? Homeless, famous, gay, mad, whatever. If they ever again run in 7 more favorites on a 9 race card, I'm going to start doing something else. Jogging. Or the museums. Or finger painting. Or chess. I mean, hell, that's just as stupid.

"FOR INSTANCE, EVERY DAY AS I DRIVE TO THE TRACK I KEEP PUNCHING THE RADIO TO DIFFERENT STATIONS LOOKING FOR MUSIC, DECENT MUSIC. IT'S ALL BAD, FLAT, LIFELESS, TUNELESS, LISTLESS."

2/27/93   12:56 AM

The captain is out to lunch and the sailors have taken over the ship.

Why are there so few interesting people? Out of the millions, why aren't there a few? Must we continue to live with this drab and ponderous species? Seems their only act is Violence. They are so good at that. They truly blossom. Shit flowers, stinking up our chance. Problem is, I must continue to interact with them. That is, if I want the lights to go on, if I want this computer repaired, if I want to flush the toilet, buy a new tire, get a tooth pulled or my gut cut open, I must continue to interact. I need the fuckers for the minute necessities, even if they, themselves, appall me. And appall is a kind word.

But they pound on my consciousness with their failure in vital areas. For instance, every day as I drive to the track I keep punching the radio to different stations looking for music, decent music. It's all bad, flat, lifeless, tuneless, listless. Yet some of these compositions sell in the millions and their creators consider themselves true Artists. It's horrible, horrible drivel entering the minds of young heads. They like it. Christ, hand them shit, they eat it up. Can't they discern? Can't they hear? Can't they feel the dilution, the staleness?

I can't believe that there is nothing. I keep punching in new stations. I've had my car less than a year yet the button I push has the black paint completely worn off. It is white, ivory-like, staring at me.

Well, yes, there is classical music. I finally have to settle for that. But I know that is always there for me. I listen to that 3 or 4 hours a night. But I still keep searching for other music. It's just not there. It should be there. It disturbs me. We've been cheated out of a whole other area. Think of all the people alive who have never heard decent music. No wonder their faces are falling off, no wonder they kill thoughtlessly, no wonder the heart is missing.

Well, what can I do? Nothing.

The movies are just as bad. I will listen to or read the critics. A great movie, they will say. And I will go see said movie. And sit there feeling like a fucking fool, feeling robbed, tricked. I can guess each scene before it arrives. And the obvious motives of the characters, what drives them, what they yearn for, what is of importance to them is so juvenile and pathetic, so boringly gross. The love bits are galling, old hat, precious drivel.

I believe that most people see too many movies. And certainly the critics. When they say that a movie is great, they mean it's great in relation to other movies they have seen. They've lost their overview. They are clubbed by more and more new movies. They just don't know, they are lost in it all. They have forgotten what really stinks, which is almost everything they view.

And let's not even talk about television.

And as a writer ... am I one? Oh well. As a writer I have trouble reading other writing. It just isn't there for me. To begin with, they don't know how to lay down a line, a paragraph. Just looking at the print from a distance, it looks boring. And when you really get down there, it's worse than boring. There's no pace. There's nothing startling or fresh. There's no gamble, no fire, no juice. What are they doing? It looks like hard work. No wonder most writers say writing is painful to them. I can understand that.

Sometimes with my writing, when it hasn't roared, I have attempted other things. I have poured wine on the pages, I have held the pages to a match and burned holes in them. "What are you DOING in there? I smell smoke!"

"No, it's all right, baby, it's all right ..."

Once my wastebasket caught fire and I rushed it out on my little balcony, poured beer over it.

For my own writing, I like to watch the boxing matches, watch how the left jab is used, the overhand right, the left hook, the uppercut, the counter punch. I like to watch them dig in, come off the canvas. There is something to be learned, something to be applied to the art of writing, the way of writing. You have just one chance and then it's gone. There are only pages left, you might as well make them smoke.

Classical music, cigars, the computer make the writing dance, holler, laugh. The nightmare life helps too.

Each day as I walk into that racetrack I know that I am blasting my hours to shit. But I still have the night. What do other writers do? Stand before the mirror and examine their ear lobes? And then write about them. Or their mothers. Or how to Save the World. Well, they can save it for me by not writing that dull stuff. That slack and withered drivel. Stop! Stop! Stop! I need something to read. Isn't there anything to read? I don't think so. If you find it, let me know. No don't. I know: you wrote it. Forget it. Go take a dump.

I remember a long raging letter I got one day from a

man who told me I had no right to say that I didn't like Shakespeare. Too many youths would believe me and just not bother to read Shakespeare. I had no right to take this stance. On and on about that. I didn't answer him. But I will here.

Screw you, buddy. And I don't like Tolstoy either!

CHARLES BUKOWSKI is one of America's best-known contemporary writers of poetry and prose, and, many would claim, its most influential and imitated poet. He was born in Andernach, Germany, to an American soldier father and a German mother in 1920, and brought to the United States at the age of three. He was raised in Los Angeles and lived there for fifty years. He published his first story in 1944 when he was twenty-four and began writing poetry at the age of thirty-five. He died in San Pedro, California, on March 9, 1994, at the age of seventy-three, shortly after completing his last novel, *Pulp* (1994).

During his lifetime he published more than forty-five books of poetry and prose, including the novels *Post Office* (1971), *Factotum* (1975), *Women* (1978), *Ham on Rye* (1982), and *Hollywood* (1989). Among his most recent books are the posthumous editions of *What Matters Most Is How Well You Walk Through the Fire* (1999), *Open All Night: New Poems* (2000), *Beerspit Night and Cursing: The Correspondence of Charles Bukowski and Sheri Martinelli 1960–1967* (2001), and *The Night Torn Mad with Footsteps: New Poems* (2001).

All of his books have now been published in translation in over a dozen languages and his worldwide popularity remains undiminished. In the years to come, Ecco will publish additional volumes of previously uncollected poetry and letters.

THESE AND OTHER TITLES BY CHARLES BUKOWSKI
ARE AVAILABLE FROM

ecco An Imprint of HarperCollinsPublishers

ISBN 0-06-057705-3 (hc)
ISBN 0-06-057706-1 (pb)

ISBN 0-06-057703-7 (hc)
ISBN 0-06-057704-5 (pb)

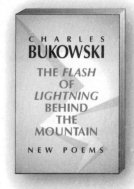

ISBN 0-06-057701-0 (hc)
ISBN 0-06-057702-9 (pb)

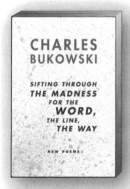

ISBN 0-06-052735-8 (hc)
ISBN 0-06-056823-2 (pb)

ISBN 0-876-85557-5 (pb)

ISBN 0-876-85362-9 (pb)

ISBN 0-876-85086-7 (pb)

ISBN 0-876-85926-0 (pb)

ISBN 0-876-85390-4 (pb)

Available wherever books are sold, or call 1-800-331-3761 to order.
www.eccobooks.com

 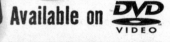